14×11

Praise for Donita K. Paul's
DragonKeeper Chronicles and Chiril Chronicles

"The writing is crisp and the setting imaginative. This series will speak to all ages of Christian readers."
—*Publisher's Weekly*

"Donita K. Paul never fails to satisfy the imagination and delight the soul.... This is fantasy that truly illuminates reality."
—JIM DENNEY, author of the Timebenders series

"Donita K. Paul's vivid imagery and startling plot twists will delight fans."
—KACY BARNETT-GRAMCKOW, author of the Genesis trilogy

"I wouldn't expect anything less from Donita K. Paul, as she always gives us a delightful read: intriguing, challenging, and full of blessing."
—KATHRYN MACKEL, author of *Vanished*

"Donita K. Paul possesses a unique talent for instilling deep wisdom and spiritual truth in a story that is engrossing and satisfying.... She is one of my favorite authors."
—HANNAH ALEXANDER, author of *Silent Pledge*

"Donita K. Paul's inventiveness never ceases to amaze. Fresh ideas for new races of people and unusual creatures keep flowing from her gifted pen."

—JILL ELIZABETH NELSON, author of the To Catch a Thief series

"Shut your eyes, hold your breath, and plunge into the unshackled imagination of Donita K. Paul."

—LINDA WICHMAN, author of *Legend of the Emerald Rose*

Two Tickets to the Christmas Ball

Two Tickets to the Christmas Ball

A Novella

Donita K. Paul

WATERBROOK
PRESS

TWO TICKETS TO THE CHRISTMAS BALL
PUBLISHED BY WATERBROOK PRESS
12265 Oracle Boulevard, Suite 200
Colorado Springs, Colorado 80921

Scripture quotations are taken from the King James Version and the Holy Bible, New International Version®. NIV®. Copyright © 1973, 1978, 1984 by Biblica Inc.™ Used by permission of Zondervan. All rights reserved worldwide. www.zondervan.com.

The characters and events in this book are fictional, and any resemblance to actual persons or events is coincidental.

ISBN 978-0-307-45899-5
ISBN 978-0-307-45900-8 (electronic)

Copyright © 2010 by Donita K. Paul

Published in association with the literary agency of Alive Communications Inc., 7680 Goddard Street, Suite 200, Colorado Springs, CO 80920, www.alive communications.com.

Published in the United States by WaterBrook Multnomah, an imprint of the Crown Publishing Group, a division of Random House Inc., New York.

WATERBROOK and its deer colophon are registered trademarks of Random House Inc.

Library of Congress Cataloging-in-Publication Data
Paul, Donita K.
    Two tickets to the Christmas ball : a novella / Donita K. Paul. — 1st ed.
        p. cm.
    ISBN 978-0-307-45899-5 — ISBN 978-0-307-45900-8 (electronic)
    1. Single women—Fiction. 2. Christmas stories. I. Title.
    PS3616.A94T96 2010
    813'.6—dc22
                        2010024543

Printed in the United States of America
2010—First Edition

10 9 8 7 6 5 4 3 2 1

This book is dedicated to:

Jessica Agius
Hannah Johnson
Rachael Selk
Becca Wilber

1

Christmas. Cora had been trying to catch it for four years. She scurried down the sidewalk, thankful that streetlights and brightly lit storefronts counteracted the gloom of early nightfall. Somewhere, sometime, she'd get ahold of how to celebrate Christmas. Maybe even tonight.

With snowflakes sticking to her black coat, Christmas lights blinking around shop windows, and incessant bells jingling, Cora should have felt some holiday cheer.

And she did.

Really.

Just not much.

At least she was on a Christmas errand this very minute. One present for a member of the family. Shouldn't that count for a bit of credit in the Christmas-spirit department?

Cora planned out her Christmas gift giving in a reasonable manner. The execution of her purchasing schedule gave her a great deal of satisfaction. Tonight's quest was a book for Uncle Eric—something about knights and castles, sword fights, shining armor, and all that.

One or two gifts purchased each week from Labor Day until December 15, and her obligations were discharged efficiently, economically, and without the excruciating last-minute frenzy that descended upon other people…like her three sisters, her mother, her grandmother, her aunts.

Cora refused to behave like her female relatives and had decided not to emulate the male side of the family either. The men didn't buy gifts. They sometimes exchanged bottles from the liquor store, but more often they drank the spirits themselves.

Her adult ambition had been to develop her own traditions for the season, ones that sprouted from the Christianity she'd discovered in college. The right way to celebrate the birth of Christ. She avoided the chaos that could choke Christmas. Oh dear. Judgmental again. At least now she recognized when she slipped.

She glanced around Sage Street. Not too many shoppers. The

quaint old shops were decked out for the holidays, but not with LED bulbs and inflated cartoon figures.

Since discovering Christianity, she'd been confused about the trappings of Christmas—the gift giving, the nativity scenes, the carols, even the Christmas tree. Every year she tried to acquire some historical background on the festivities. She was learning. She had hope. But she hadn't wrapped her head around all the traditions yet.

The worst part was shopping.

Frenzy undid her. Order sustained her. And that was a good reason to steer clear of any commercialized holiday rush. She'd rather screw red light bulbs into plastic reindeer faces than push through a crowd of shoppers.

Cora examined the paper in her hand and compared it to the address above the nearest shop. Number 483 on the paper and 527 on the building. Close.

When she'd found the bookstore online, she had been amazed that a row of old-fashioned retailers still existed a few blocks from the high-rise office building where she worked. Truthfully, it was more like the bookstore found her. Every time she opened her browser, and on every site she visited, the ad for the old-fashioned new- and used-book store showed up in a banner or sidebar. She'd asked around, but none of her co-workers patronized the Sage Street Shopping District.

"Sounds like a derelict area to me," said Meg, the receptionist. "Sage Street is near the old railroad station, isn't it? The one they decided was historic so they wouldn't tear it down, even though it's empty and an eyesore?"

An odd desire to explore something other than the mall near her apartment seized Cora. "I'm going to check it out."

Jake, the security guard, frowned at her. "Take a cab. You don't want to be out too late over there."

Cora walked. The brisk air strengthened her lungs, right? The exercise pumped her blood, right? A cab would cost three, maybe four dollars, right?

An old man, sitting on the stoop of a door marked 503, nodded at her. She smiled, and he winked as he gave her a toothless grin. Startled, she quickened her pace and gladly joined the four other pedestrians waiting at the corner for the light to change.

Number 497 emblazoned the window of an ancient shoe store on the opposite corner. She marched on. In this block she'd find the book and check another item off her Christmas list.

Finally! "Warner, Werner, and Wizbotterdad, Books," Cora read the sign aloud and then grasped the shiny knob. It didn't turn. She frowned. Stuck? Locked? The lights were on. She pressed her face against the glass. A man sat at the counter. Reading. How appropriate.

Cora wrenched the knob. A gust of wind pushed with her

against the door, and she blew into the room. She stumbled and straightened, and before she could grab the door and close it properly, it swung closed, without the loud bang she expected.

"I don't like loud noises," the man said without looking up from his book.

"Neither do I," said Cora.

He nodded over his book. With one gnarled finger, he pushed his glasses back up his nose.

Must be an interesting book. Cora took a quick look around. The place could use stronger lights. She glanced back at the clerk. His bright lamp cast him and his book in a golden glow.

Should she peruse the stacks or ask?

She decided to browse. She started to enter the aisle between two towering bookcases.

"Not there," said the old man.

"I beg your pardon?" said Cora.

"How-to books. How to fix a leaky faucet. How to build a bridge. How to mulch tomatoes. How to sing opera. How-to books. You don't need to know any of that, do you?"

"No."

"Wrong aisle, then." He placed the heavy volume on the counter and leaned over it, apparently absorbed once more.

Cora took a step toward him. "I think I saw a movie like this once."

His head jerked up, his scowl heavier. He glared over the top of his glasses at the books on the shelves as if they had suddenly moved or spoken or turned bright orange.

"A movie? Here? I suppose you mean the backdrop of a bookstore. Not so unusual." He arched an eyebrow. *"You've Got Mail* and *84 Charing Cross Road."*

"I meant the dialogue. You spoke as if you knew what I needed."

He hunched his shoulders. The dark suspenders stretched across the faded blue of his shirt. "Reading customers. Been in the business a long time."

"I'm looking for a book for my uncle. He likes castles, knights, tales of adventure. That sort of thing."

He sighed, closed his book, and tapped its cover. "This is it." He stood as Cora came to the desk. "Do you want me to wrap it and send it? We have the service. My grandson's idea."

Cora schooled her face and her voice. One of the things she excelled in was not showing her exasperation. She'd been trained by a dysfunctional family, and that had its benefits. She knew how to take guff and not give it back. Maintaining a calm attitude was a good job skill.

She tried a friendly smile and addressed the salesclerk.

"I want to look at it first and find out how much it costs."

"It's the book you want, and the price is eleven dollars and thirteen cents."

Cora rubbed her hand over the cover. It looked and felt like leather, old leather, but in good repair. The book must be ancient.

"Are you sure?" she asked.

"Which?" the old man barked.

"Which what?"

"Which part of the statement am I sure about? It doesn't matter because I'm sure about both."

Cora felt her armor of detachment suffer a dent. The man was impossible. She could probably order a book online and get it wrapped and delivered right to her uncle with less aggravation. But dollar signs blinked in neon red in her mind as she thought how much that would cost. No need to be hasty.

Curtain rings rattled on a rod, and Cora looked up to see a younger version of the curmudgeon step into the area behind the counter.

The younger man smiled. He had the same small, wiry build as the older version, but his smile was warm and genuine. He looked to be about fifty, but his hair was still black, as black as the old man's hair was white. He stretched out his hand, and Cora shook it.

"I'm Bill Wizbotterdad. This is my granddad, William Wizbotterdad."

"Let me guess. Your father is named Will?"

Bill grinned, obviously pleased she'd caught on quickly. "*Willie* Wizbotterdad. He's off in Europe collecting rare books."

"He's not!" said the elder shop owner.

"He is." Bill cast his granddad a worried look.

"That's just the reason he gave for not being here." William shook his head and leaned across the counter. "He doesn't like Christmas. We have a special job to do at Christmas, and he doesn't like people and dancing and matrimony."

Bill put his arm around his grandfather and pulled him back. He let go of his granddad and spun the book on the scarred wooden counter so that Cora could read the contents. "Take a look." He opened the cover and flipped through the pages. "Colored illustrations."

A rattling of the doorknob was followed by the sound of a shoulder thudding against the wood. Cora turned to see the door fly open with a tall man attached to it. The stranger brushed snow from his sleeves, then looked up at the two shop owners. Cora caught them giving each other a smug smile, a wink, and a nod of the head.

Odd. Lots of oddness in this shop.

She liked the book, and she wanted to leave before more snow accumulated on the streets. Yet something peculiar about this shop and the two men made her curious. Part of her longed to linger. However, smart girls trusted their instincts and didn't hang around places that oozed mystery. She didn't feel threatened, just intrigued. But getting to know the peculiar booksellers better was the last thing she wanted, right? She needed to get home and be done with this Christmas shopping business. "I'll take the book."

The newcomer stomped his feet on the mat by the door, then took off his hat.

Cora did a double take. "Mr. Derrick!"

He cocked his head and scrunched his face. "Do I know you?" The man was handsome, even wearing that comical lost expression. "Excuse me. Have we met?"

"We work in the same office."

He studied her a moment, and a look of recognition lifted the frown. "Third desk on the right." He hesitated, then snapped his fingers. "Cora Crowden."

"Crowder."

He jammed his hand in his pocket, moving his jacket aside. His tie hung loosely around his neck. She'd never seen him looking relaxed. The office clerks called him Serious Simon Derrick.

"I drew your name," she said.

He looked puzzled.

"For the gift exchange. Tomorrow night. Office party."

"Oh. Of course." He nodded. "I drew Mrs. Hudson. She's going to retire, and I heard her say she wanted to redecorate on a shoestring."

"That's Mrs. Wilson. Mrs. Hudson is taking leave to be with her daughter, who is giving birth to triplets."

He frowned and began looking at the books.

"You won't be there, will you?" Cora asked.

"At the party? No, I never come."

"I know. I mean, I've worked at Sorenby's for five years, and you've never been there."

The puzzled expression returned to Serious Simon's face. He glanced to the side. "I'm looking for the how-to section."

Cora grinned. "On your left. Second aisle."

He turned to stare at her, and she pointed to the shelves Mr. Wizbotterdad had not let her examine. Mr. Derrick took a step in that direction.

Cora looked back at the shop owners and caught them leaning back in identical postures, grins on their faces, and arms crossed over their chests.

Bill jerked away from the wall, grabbed her book, rummaged below the counter, and brought out a bag. He slid the book inside, then looked at her. "You didn't want the book wrapped and delivered?"

"No, I'll just pay for it now."

"Are you sure you wouldn't like to look around some more?" asked Bill.

"Right," said William. "No hurry. Look around. Browse. You might find something you like."

Bill elbowed William.

Simon Derrick had disappeared between the stacks.

William nodded toward the how-to books. "Get a book. We have a copy of *How to Choose Gifts for Ungrateful Relatives.* Third from the bottom shelf, second case from the wall."

The statement earned him a "sh" from his grandson.

Cora shifted her attention to the man from her office and walked a few paces to peek around the shelves. "Mr. Derrick, I'm getting ready to leave. If you're not coming to the party, may I just leave the gift on your desk tomorrow?"

He glanced at her before concentrating again on the many books. "That's fine. Nice to see you, Miss Crowden."

"Crowder," she corrected, but he didn't answer.

She went to the counter and paid. Mr. Derrick grunted when she said good-bye at the door.

"Come back again," said Bill.

"Yes," said William. "We have all your heart's desires."

Bill elbowed him, and Cora escaped into the blustering weather.

She hiked back to the office building. Snow sprayed her with tiny crystals, and the sharp wind nipped her nose. Inside the parking garage, warm air helped her thaw a bit as she walked to the spot she leased by the month. It would be a long ride home on slippery roads. But once she arrived, there would be no one there to interrupt her plans. She got in the car, turned the key, pushed the gearshift into reverse, looked over her shoulder, and backed out of her space.

She would get the gift ready to mail off and address a few cards in the quiet of her living room. There would be no yelling. That's what she liked about living states away from her family. No one would ambush her with complaints and arguments when she walked through the door.

Except Skippy. Skippy waited. One fat, getting fatter, cat to talk to. She did complain at times about her mistress being gone too long, about her dinner being late, about things Cora could not fathom. But Cora never felt condemned by Skippy, just prodded a little.

Once inside her second-floor apartment, she pulled off her gloves, blew her nose, and went looking for Skippy.

The cat was not behind the curtain, sitting on the window seat, staring at falling snow. Not in her closet, curled up in a boot she'd knocked over. Not in the linen closet, sleeping on clean towels. She wasn't in any of her favorite spots. Cora looked around and saw the paper bag that, this morning, had been filled with wadded scraps of Christmas paper. Balls of pretty paper and bits of ribbon littered the floor. There. Cora bent over and spied her calico cat in the bag.

"Did you have fun, Skippy?"

The cat rolled on her back and batted the top of the paper bag. Skippy then jumped from her cave and padded after Cora, as her owner headed for the bedroom.

Thirty minutes later, Cora sat at the dining room table in her cozy pink robe that enveloped her from neck to ankles. She stirred a bowl of soup and eyed the fifteen packages she'd wrapped earlier in the week. Two more sat waiting for their ribbons.

These would cost a lot less to send if some of these people were on speaking terms. She could box them together and ship them off in large boxes.

She spooned chicken and rice into her mouth and swallowed. The soup was a tad too hot. She kept stirring.

She could send one package with seven gifts inside to Grandma Peterson, who could dispense them to her side of the family. She could send three to Aunt Carol.

She took another sip. Cooler.

Aunt Carol could keep her gift and give two to her kids. She could send five to her mom…

Cora grimaced. She had three much older sisters and one younger. "If Mom were on speaking terms with my sisters, that would help."

She eyed Skippy, who had lifted a rear leg to clean between her back toes. "You don't care, do you? Well, I'm trying to. And I think I'm doing a pretty good job with this Christmas thing."

She reached over and flipped the switch on her radio. A Christmas carol poured out and jarred her nerves. She really should think about Christmas and not who received the presents. *Better to think "my uncle" than "Joe, that bar bum and pool shark."*

She finished her dinner, watching her cat wash her front paws.

"You and I need to play. You're"—she paused as Skippy turned a meaningful glare at her—"getting a bit rotund, dear kitty."

Skippy sneezed and commenced licking her chest.

After dinner, Cora curled up on the couch with her Warner,

Werner, and Wizbotterdad bag. Skippy came to investigate the rattling paper.

Uncle Eric. Uncle Eric used to recite "You Are Old, Father William." He said it was about a knight. But Cora wasn't so sure. She dredged up memories from college English. The poem was by Lewis Carroll, who was really named Dodson, Dogson, Dodgson, or something.

"He wrote *Alice's Adventures in Wonderland*," she said. "There's a cat in the story, but not as fine a cat as you. He smiles too much."

Skippy gave her a squint-eyed look.

Cora eased the leather-bound book out of the bag. "The William I met at the bookstore qualifies for at least ancient."

She put the book in her lap and ran her fingers over the embossed title: *How the Knights Found Their Ladies.*

She might have been hasty. She didn't know if Uncle Eric would like this. She hefted the book, guessing its weight to be around four pounds. She should have found a lighter gift. This would cost a fortune to mail.

Skippy sniffed at the binding, feline curiosity piqued. Cora stroked her fur and pushed her back. She opened the book to have a peek inside. A piece of thick paper fell out. Skippy pounced on it as it twirled to the floor.

"What is it, kitty? A bookmark?" She slipped it out from between Skippy's paws, then turned the rectangle over in her hands. Not a bookmark. A ticket.

Admit one to the Wizards' Christmas Ball
Costumes required
Dinner and Dancing
and your Destiny

Never heard of it. She tucked the ticket in between the pages and continued to flip through the book, stopping to read an occasional paragraph.

This book wasn't for Uncle Eric at all. It was not a history, it was a story. Kind of romantic too. Definitely not Uncle Eric's preferred reading.

Skippy curled against her thigh and purred.

"You know what, cat? I'm going to keep it."

Skippy made her approval known by stretching her neck up and rubbing her chin on the edge of the leather cover. Cora put the book on the sofa and picked up Skippy for a cuddle. The cat squirmed out of her arms, batted at the ticket sticking out of the pages, and scampered off.

"I love you too," called Cora.

She pulled the ticket out and read it again: *Wizards' Christmas Ball.* She turned out the light and headed for bed. But as she got ready, her eye caught the computer on her desk. Maybe she could find a bit more information.

2

Simon Derrick stepped out of his snow-packed boots and tiptoed in his stocking feet through the kitchen to the living room. The floorboards under the old green linoleum creaked under his weight. None of his family members looked up from their projects. He placed an armload of chopped wood in the box beside the fireplace.

"Simon, singing?" Sandy's round face wore her thinking-very-hard expression. The corners of her almond-shaped eyes, typical of Down syndrome, crinkled behind pretty pink spectacle frames. Laughing or thinking, she always looked like a pixie. She kept telling Simon she would be twenty-five in January, and therefore could no longer be a pixie. They hadn't been able to decide what she should be next. He wanted her to stay his pixie.

She pointed her pencil at him. "Singing?"

As he took off his coat, he grinned at his sister. "I know what messed you up, Sandy. Ready? S-I-N-G." He paused, waiting for her to get the letters down on her Christmas card. When she looked up, he added, "I-N-G."

She shook her head, straight brown locks of hair swinging around her face. "I already did I-N-G."

"Two of them?"

She shook her head.

"Sing-ing." He took care to pronounce each syllable distinctly. "There's two."

Sandy giggled. "It doesn't sound like that."

"Of course not. Singing should sound like this." He stood straighter, placed one hand on his chest and extended the other. He let out his best operatic bellow. "Away in a manger—"

"Stop!" Covering her ears, his mother turned from the jigsaw puzzle she was doing with Grandpa John. "You're ruining a beautiful carol."

"Yes, enough of that silliness. I want to really sing," said Aunt Mae. "It's just what we need." She struggled up from her seat and trotted across the room to grab her guitar.

"No hippie music," shouted Grandpa John.

Simon grinned as he went to pull Aunt Mae's stool from the

closet. Great-aunt Mae was older than her brother John but acted younger. She said it was all the yogurt and whole grains. Skinny as a rail, with long gray hair hanging straight down her back, she wore long skirts, huge blouses, and sandals. In winter she wore sandals with colorful socks she'd knitted. She also made hemp belts and lots of jewelry from stones. She had belonged to a folk-singing troupe in the sixties.

She scowled at her brother and shouted, "Christmas music."

Grandpa John waved a hand at her. "That's fine, then."

Simon sat on the arm of the couch. Sandy gathered two instruments, a harmonica and a beatnik drum, and came to sit on the sofa near her brother. Simon's mother played the piano to accompany Aunt Mae's guitar. Sandy played the bongo, and she kept a neat beat. Simon played the harmonica.

He soaked up the warmth of the fire and the joy of being with his family as they sang carols. These songs that brought back memories of years and years of celebrating the birth of Christ. The family had lost a few members over the years: his father, his brother, two uncles—all deceased. Simon glanced around and reminded himself to cherish what he had.

Sandy yawned several times during "Silent Night." At the end of the song, before his mom had a chance to start another carol, he whisked his little sister's drum away. "Time for bed."

She made a face. "I'm twenty-four. You don't have to send me to bed."

"I'm not sending you to bed, Candy-Sandy. I bought you a new book today, and I don't want you to go to sleep before we read it."

The speed with which she kissed and hugged everyone good night didn't surprise him. Books motivated her even better than sweets, and Sandy did like sweets. She scooted up the stairs. He hardly had time to bank the fire before she called down. "I'm ready."

He said good night, grabbed the bag from Warner, Werner, and Wizbotterdad, and climbed the stairs. Sandy was tucked in bed, leaning against a stack of pillows, waiting for him with her stuffed hippopotamus. The hippo wore a rainbow-colored crocheted dress with beads woven into the hemline.

"Is the book about a kitten?" she asked.

He shook his head. Sandy wanted a kitten for Christmas, but he wasn't going to be lured into a discussion of cats tonight.

"Two kittens?"

He pulled up his chair, opened the bag, and took out two books.

"Two books?" Sandy sat straighter. "Is one about a kitten?"

"No. This one is for a Mrs. Hudson at work. I drew her name for the Christmas gift exchange."

"What's her book about?"

"*The Care and Feeding of Triplets.* Mrs. Hudson's daughter is going to have three babies."

Sandy's eyes grew big, and Simon wondered what she was thinking. He knew better than to ask. She could back him into corners he didn't want to be in with her innocent questions. He plunged into a description of the odd bookshop.

"The older Mr. Wizbotterdad went down the aisle of how-to books, muttering something that sounded like 'care and fuh-duh-wuhp igless.' He'd tap the books, pull volumes halfway out, and then shove them in again, all the time saying, 'care and fuh-duh-wuhp igless,' 'care and fuh-duh-wuhp igless.'"

Sandy giggled.

"Then he pulled out a book like he'd finally found a treasure and handed it to me."

"This one?" said Sandy.

"No, not this one. It was a different book. *The Care and Feeding of Piglets.*"

Sandy laughed out loud, rolling in her bed and hugging Henrietta the Hippie Hippo. When she settled down, she had slipped deeper under the covers, and her head rested on the pillow.

She yawned. "Are you going to read?"

He opened the other book from the shop. A rectangular paper fell out. He bent to pick it up.

"What's that?" Sandy stirred.

He flipped it over. "Just a bookmark."

"May I see it?"

He handed it to his little sister.

She scrutinized it with a frown. "It doesn't have any pictures." She handed it back. "I'm too tired to read it, Simon."

"And you don't have your glasses on." He took it and turned it over a couple of times. It said the same thing on the front and back. He read aloud. " 'Admit one to the Wizards' Christmas Ball. Costumes required. Dinner and Dancing and your Destiny.' "

"It's a ticket." Sandy sat up. "To a ball."

"It's probably just an advertisement for something."

"I'd like to go to a ball."

"But there's no day. No time. No location."

"You could look it up on the Internet. You could find it."

"I'll look after you go to sleep. Lie down again," he said. "I promise to look. Now, do you want me to read?"

"Yes." Sandy snuggled under the covers and hugged her hippo.

"Are you warm enough?"

She nodded.

He opened the book again. "Once upon a time, there were two people, a man and a woman, who spent every day in the same office. They didn't *really* know each other. Sometimes, he couldn't even remember her name.

"He was happy, but not as happy as God wanted…"

He flipped the book closed and looked at the back. He opened to the copyright page and found that an obscure company had published the book.

"What's the matter?" Sandy yawned again. "Are there pictures?"

He turned the book around and held it close to Sandy so she

could see a picture of a castle with many workers busy doing their jobs.

She nodded. "Why did you stop?"

"The book's a Christian book, and I didn't know it."

"That's not bad. We love Jesus."

"No, definitely not bad. I just didn't know that." Simon turned the book around to continue reading.

Sandy rolled onto her side. "What's the name? You forgot to tell me the name."

"How This Knight Found His Fair Lady."

"Read."

Simon nodded. "He was happy, but not as happy as God wanted him to be. He was busy, but not always busy doing what God wanted him to do. He didn't know it, but God was about to do something about those two things."

He looked up and watched Sandy breathe deeply, eyes closed. A pixie. A kindhearted, organized, levelheaded pixie. She didn't read or spell very well, and you could forget math altogether. But as long as she was at home, he knew Grandpa would get his medicine on time, Mom would stop crocheting her doll dresses long enough to get dinner, and Aunt Mae would get out of bed in the morning, shower, and get dressed.

The last was a big responsibility. Once Aunt Mae was up, the elderly woman ran on full steam. But unless someone prodded her out of bed, she'd stay there. The longer she stayed there, the harder it was to get her up.

He stuck the ticket in the book and set the book on Sandy's nightstand. He pushed the chair back and reached to turn out her little lamp. Light shot from the circle in the top of the shade and illuminated an embroidered sampler with the words *Be brave and try new things* stitched onto it. Sandy had decided it was the family motto. Sometimes he marveled at her bravery.

"Don't forget about my kitten," Sandy called, her eyes still closed.

He sighed as he went out the door. He didn't shut it all the way because having the door closed scared his very special sister. He'd have to find a kitten before Christmas.

Simon got ready for bed and sat down at his desk in his room. His face and T-shirt were reflected in the computer screen. For Christmas he wanted to replace his old computer and get one with an antiglare monitor. With a few clicks, he'd opened a search engine.

He typed "Wizards' Christmas Ball" in the little box.

The Web site came up quickly.

December 23, 8:00 p.m., Melchior Hotel. The address was on the same street as those funny shops.

Must have a ticket to attend. Well, that seemed obvious. It would be fun to take Sandy.

Must wear costume befitting a ballroom dance. Sandy would love that.

He continued to read. Frowning, he started at the top and scrolled down to the bottom. Who put this shindig on? Where were you supposed to get these tickets? He clicked on another page. Pictures of past balls changed in a well-designed slide show. Several people stood around in wizard robes with tall hats, and women wore fancy ball gowns. It looked like everyone was having fun. But there was no information about how to purchase a ticket.

He clicked through to a page that showed sponsors for the ball. All of them were stores on Sage Street.

Aha! *Warner, Werner, and Wizbotterdad.* The bookstore was a sponsor. He'd go back and get another ticket there.

He closed the site, and while he moved the cursor down to click Start, he saw in the monitor his light blue T-shirt turn pink. He squinted and leaned forward.

Instead of his reflection, he saw a woman's face. She was squinting and leaning toward the screen. He jumped back, and so did she. He blinked, and it was him again.

Definitely him in his blue T-shirt.

He shut down the machine. Weird. Was it a ghost image from a site trying to load? He'd never heard of a ghost image. He shook his head, swiped his hand down his face, and pushed away from the desk.

He was tired. Just tired.

Cora found a Web site for the ball. The pictures of previous balls looked intriguing, but everyone in them had a partner. Couple after couple gazed into each other's eyes as they danced, sat at tables smiling and laughing, and held hands as they walked from the beautiful ballroom backdrop to the intimate tables.

Cora couldn't see herself, *by* herself, enjoying such an affair. And she didn't have a dress. Every woman in the photos wore a glamorous costume that shimmered and sparkled. This extravaganza was for the rich and romantic, right? And she was poor and pragmatic, right?

She sighed and moved her mouse so the arrow hovered over the *X* in the upper right-hand corner. An image of a man hung in the background on her computer screen. She leaned forward, and the image seemed to lean forward as well. A reflection in the mirror would have responded exactly the same, except a mirror would have shown her female face, not the vague impression of a sleepy man.

She jerked back. Webcam? Her computer didn't have a webcam, did it? She exited the site.

Wizards' balls were not up her alley. Apparently Web sites for wizards' balls were a challenge to logical thinking.

A fluke, that's all.

She went to the living room to throw the ticket away. She didn't know why it was important to chuck it in the trash immediately, but it was.

No ticket. Not in the book. Not on the coffee table. Not under the cushions of the couch.

Cora went to the bathroom to brush her teeth, and the ticket was on the floor next to her plush rug. Obviously Skippy had carried it in. She picked it up and threw it in the trash.

Gratefully, she went to bed. Her warm covers provided a cozy haven against odd, old men, socially inept executives, tickets to balls, and phantoms in her computer.

Morning brought sunshine, but Cora struggled with heaviness in her spirit. That wasn't surprising. She just didn't know what to do with Christmas. And Skippy was in hiding. Cora had no company at breakfast, and the cat refused to come out, even as she grabbed her purse and dug out her keys.

As she headed toward the door, Cora noticed that the ball ticket sat on the counter in the kitchen, next to the coffeepot. Unsettling, but not the end of the world. The cat playing tricks. Nothing more than that.

Then, on the way into work, her car slid on a patch of ice and tried to level a curb. The curb did not yield, but her tire did. Rather, something connecting the tire to the axle yielded.

Her car had to be towed.

When she finally made it into the office, Cora grabbed her stack of files and hightailed it to the meeting that had started an hour before. With the files clenched to her chest, she knocked softly and entered the conference room.

Mrs. Hudson jumped up. "Are you all right, dear? Did you get a jolt?" Cora had called in while she was waiting for the tow truck, so Mrs. Hudson, her supervisor, knew why she was late. "Sometimes the pain shows up in your neck and shoulders the day after the accident."

"I'm fine." Cora laid her files on the table.

"Your car?" asked the department head, Jeff Stockton.

"Insured."

"Deductible?"

"Five hundred."

Harry, the accountant, scrunched up his face. "Ouch."

"Right before Christmas. What a bummer," said Lisa, the statistics queen.

Mrs. Hudson patted Cora's arm. "We'll talk after the meeting."

Cora took her seat. Jeff pushed a paper-clipped stack of documents at her, and the team went back on task. Cora said a prayer. She needed to concentrate. The accident had rattled her, but the real problem was her missing cat. Skippy played her hide-and-seek game daily, but she always came to say good-bye as Cora left for work. Where was that cat?

3

Simon Derrick smacked the steering wheel with his hand. He turned the corner and cruised the street one more time. Sage Street had disappeared. He looked at his watch. He didn't have any more time to drive around the same nine blocks in a three-by-three grid, looking for a side street that didn't want to be found.

He turned at the next light to hit the freeway. He'd try again after his lunch. He didn't want to keep Pastor Greg Spencer waiting.

Three cars sat in the restaurant parking lot. Spence picked their weekly rendezvous point from a coupon book the youth group sold every year. Sometimes they lucked out and the food was actually edible.

Simon parked his car, strolled into Little Leland's Tex-Mex Diner, and sniffed. The restaurant passed the first and second tests. He hated places where dim lights hid grimy floors. Leland's lights shone over polished tabletops and sparkling-clean water glasses. And the fragrance of the place indicated spices, not heavy fried grease. A plus.

Spence sat in a booth, talking to a blond waitress. He spotted Simon and waved him over. The waitress held her pencil poised above a pad of paper.

His friend pointed to the menu. "I ordered nachos for an appetizer."

Simon nodded. "Sounds good. I'll have a bean and beef burrito, a quesadilla, and two beef tacos, please. And hot tea."

"You don't want to see a menu?" asked the blonde.

"No time, I'm late. And that's what I would end up ordering anyway. That's what I like."

"Okay." She turned toward the kitchen. "I'll be back with your drinks and the nachos."

"So why is my Johnny-on-the-spot friend late?" asked the pastor. "Traffic?"

"Trying to find a bookstore—no, a whole street—that I walked down yesterday. Today, it's gone."

"What street? Where?"

Simon shrugged out of his coat and hung it on a hook. "Sage."

"Sage runs right in front of the old railroad station."

"I found that part. This store was about five blocks west of the station."

Spence shook his head. "Sage stops at Bessell. Dead-ends."

"No, it jogs."

"It's not a part of town I'm familiar with, but I'm pretty sure that section of Sage perished when they built Corporate Square—fifteen, twenty years ago."

"It was there yesterday." Simon shook his head. "I bought a book at Warner, Werner, and Wizbotterdad. Actually, I bought two." He reached in his pocket and pulled out the ticket. "And they gave me this ticket."

Spence took it. "The Wizards' Christmas Ball? Where are you supposed to go for this ball? When? Who sponsors it? Why give away tickets?"

He flipped the paper in the air. Simon snatched it before it fell to the table.

"Exactly. But Sandy saw it, and she wants to go."

Spence's eyebrows rose. "I see."

"Yeah, I know you do."

The server brought a hot tea and a coffee, a basket of chips, and a small bowl of salsa.

"Nachos will be here in a sec." She swirled away to take orders from another table.

Spence prayed. Then Simon scooped up a blob of hot red sauce to shove in his mouth. "Mmm-mmm." He spoke around crunching corn chips. "This may be one of your better finds, my man."

They devoured the food when it came and, between bites, discussed church business, their families, and Christmas.

As Simon waited for his credit card, he looked at his old friend. "Her heart's not strong, you know. That pneumonia last year nearly killed her."

Spence easily picked up the original thread of conversation— Simon's concern for his sister. He nodded and looked at his hands cupped around his almost-empty coffee mug. "Sandy may outlive you."

"Yeah. Well, I like to make her happy, but there was no information on where to buy another ticket. I thought I'd go back to the bookstore." He glanced at his watch. "But I have to get back to the office. The division meetings were this morning, and by now files are stacking up on my desk."

The men stood and shook hands. Pastor Spencer's eyebrows shot up again, and he snapped his fingers. "I remember hearing something about Sage Street and a ball."

"What?"

"A crazy story from when I was in seminary."

The men walked toward the door.

"Give it to me quick," said Simon.

"Two people who ended up being a husband-wife missionary

team met at a Christmas ball. Seems to me they got their costumes at a shop on Sage. But I was in seminary twenty years ago. The whole street was still there back then."

Simon shoved the door open and let his friend pass. "Very helpful, Spence. And the street *is* still there. I'll find it."

Simon wrote instructions neatly in the margin of the fifth report. He put the pencil down and pinched the bridge of his nose. Leaning back in his office chair, he stretched his arms out to the side, then above his head. He stretched his shoulder muscles, loosening tension, then brought his arms down. He glanced out the sixth-floor office window and saw that full night had descended upon the city. His clock said a quarter after six.

He'd missed dinner at home, but Sandy would have a plate waiting to stick in the microwave. She learned such tricks from watching old TV show DVDs. His mother had been domestic while his father lived, but now she and Aunt Mae were entrepreneurs, selling crocheted doll clothes and jewelry.

The telephone rang. It was probably Sandy. He looked at caller ID and didn't recognize the number.

He picked up the receiver. "Hello?"

"Benjy here. I'm looking for Cora Crowder. I've got her—"

"No, wait," Simon interrupted, reaching for a phone list on a battered card in a vertical slot file on his desk. "You have the wrong extension. Miss Crowder is 4546."

"That's what I dialed."

"Must have been a crossed wire then." Simon shook his head. The possibility of crossed telephone wires disappeared into history long ago. The man just misdialed.

"Okay. Sorry to bother you. I'll try again."

Simon hung up.

Was Cora Crowder still in the building? Almost everyone left early on the night of the office party. This year it was at the grill across the street. He looked out of his glassed-in cubicle and saw a light at a desk down the hall. A coat hung over the back of her chair, but he didn't see Miss Crowder.

The phone rang again. The number looked similar to the one that came through only moments before. Simon grabbed the phone before it rang a second time.

"Yes?"

"Uh-oh. You're still not Miss Crowder."

"You have the same wrong extension again."

The guy gave a sigh of exasperation, but persisted without getting angry. "Look, I dialed 4546. Do you know her? I want to go eat my supper with my kids."

"I do."

"This is Benjy at Benjy's Repair Shop. She slid her car into a curb this morning, and I got her a new tie rod. Can you tell her she can come get the car? No hurry. Now that I know she'll get the message, I'm going to eat."

"Okay, I'll tell her."

"Thanks. Merry Christmas."

The phone went dead. Simon stepped out into the semidark office pool. Eight of the nine cubicles were empty, and the lights were off. Only one light was still lit, the one in Miss Crowder's cubicle. But she wasn't at her desk.

He looked in the shadows of the room and spotted Cora gazing out the window. With her arms crossed over her chest, she looked like she was either warming or protecting herself. But her shoulders slumped. Not enough tension in her body language to be in a defensive mode, so she must be chilly. The janitors had turned down the heat.

"Miss Crowder. I have a message for you."

She jumped, put her hand to her chest, and sighed. "Mr. Derrick. I thought everyone had gone to the party."

He came to stand beside her and looked down at the street below and the lights of the restaurant. "Are you wishing you were there?"

She shrugged. "A little."

"Benjy's Repair Shop called, and your car is ready."

She frowned and looked over her shoulder at her desk. "My phone didn't ring. I've been waiting for the call."

"Somehow the call came through to my desk. Twice." He puzzled over that for a moment, but the oddity really wasn't worth a concerted effort to track down the cause. If the problem persisted, he'd put someone on it. "He said you slid into a curb this morning. And he already has the car fixed for you tonight? Sounds like someone I'd like to do business with."

She laughed. "He's a friend from church. He had the part he needed in his garage under a pile of junk. He said he didn't even remember how he got it and was just fortunate to see it before he made a trip to the junkyard."

"a commercial garage?"

"Yes."

"I think I'll write down his number."

She started for her desk. "Right now I'm going to call a cab."

"Why don't you go to the party first? Benjy said there was no hurry."

She looked over her shoulder and smiled. "I usually only stay for the first hour. I'm there for the food and the gift exchange, but I don't think I'm in the mood tonight."

He nodded and turned toward his office. Before he'd passed her desk, she opened a drawer and pulled out the phone book. She placed it on the top, shoved the drawer shut with her knee, and gasped.

He stopped. "Did you hurt yourself?"

"No, I just remembered your gift. It's on the backseat of my car. I forgot all about it until just now."

"No problem."

"I'll bring it in tomorrow."

"Tomorrow is Saturday."

"Monday." She shifted from one foot to the other.

Simon ran his hand through his hair. He wanted to go home, and two more reports sat on his desk. He never took work home. But he wanted out of there, and here stood a good excuse, or that he could label as helping a neighbor.

He stuck a hand in his pocket and jingled his keys. "I'm ready to go home. Don't call the cab. I'll give you a lift to Benjy's."

Cora peeked at Simon as they took the elevator to the parking garage below the building. Serious Simon carried his briefcase. No small talk. He looked absorbed in his thoughts.

She tried to think of something to say to engage him in conversation, but then thought, *Why bother?* Simon Derrick was a nice man, but every one of the young women in the office gave him a wide berth. Mrs. Hudson said he talked about his family once in a blue moon, usually as an excuse not to do something, like go on a business trip. Cora couldn't remember ever hearing him talk about his life outside the office. Cora wondered if he chatted with his wife. Or did he stroll past their living room couch like he strolled through the office, obviously deep in thought?

Once in the bowels of the building, they walked through a maze of cement columns to the place where her car would ordinarily be sitting. Cora stopped and stared as Mr. Derrick pulled out his keys and unlocked the car in the next slot. He glanced over to where she stood, frozen.

"Something wrong?" he asked.

She pointed to her spot, number eighty-eight. "This is my parking space. Have we parked next to each other for five years?"

"No, not that long. When I renewed my lease, I lost the slot I'd had since I started here through a clerical error. That was in October."

"So you've been parking here since October?"

"Yes."

She shrugged and opened the passenger door. She didn't believe in coincidences.

They left the parking garage, and Simon turned right onto the street.

Cora frowned. "I thought I mentioned Benjy's was off the Blackton Bridge."

"Oh, I'm sorry. I should have said something, but this just popped into my mind again. I tried at noon to find Sage Street and the bookstore, but I kept making wrong turns. I thought maybe with the streets emptier, I'd have more luck."

"Do you want to return your purchase?"

"No, I want to get another of the ball tickets they're giving away. Or find out where to buy one. Did you get a ticket?"

"Yes." She thought about the pictures she'd seen on the Web site. The intriguing images couldn't lure her to attend alone. "You can have mine. I'm not interested in going."

Simon Derrick smiled, actually smiled. "Really?"

She nodded.

"Thanks. I'll take it. You wouldn't happen to be unloading kittens, would you?"

"No, I have one grown cat, but she has less of a social life than I do."

Mr. Derrick sighed. "I don't know where to find one. I called the animal shelter, but they said the older ones are all taken. The kittens they have are too young for adoption and already spoken for. Puppies too. But I don't think my household is ready for a puppy."

"How many children do you have?"

"Children?"

Did his voice squeak?

"No children. I'm not married."

"You have a family?"

"Yes. Granddad, Mom, Aunt Mae, and my sister, Sandy."

Cora's cell phone rang. She fished it out of her purse, looked at caller ID, and silenced the ringer. She poked it back in her purse with a little more force than necessary.

Mr. Derrick turned, pointing his car to the on ramp of the freeway. "Not Benjy with bad news, I hope."

"No, just one of the cast of *Tomorrow's Sorrows.*"

He frowned. "Sounds like a soap opera."

"It is."

"You have friends who are TV actors?"

"No, my family." She sighed. She never talked about her family. "They live their own soap opera. I call it *Tomorrow's Sorrows* because whatever they choose today inevitably ends up being something they regret tomorrow."

"Do you live with them?"

"No. God rescued me from their influence. Then He rescued me from the life by giving me a job at Sorenby's. I'm three wide states away from constant chaos, frenzy, and fights."

Simon didn't say anything. She didn't blame him. She sounded judgmental, complaining about her family. She was judgmental. Why had she opened her big mouth?

He drove efficiently, without any macho derring-do, the rest of the way to Benjy's. The mechanic came down and handed her the keys. She gave Benjy a check and Mr. Derrick his gift. Benjy gave her a jaunty salute, loped over to the side of the garage, and climbed the stairs that led to his home. Serious Simon Derrick held the red package with green, silver, and gold curlicues sprouting from the top.

He stared at it as if he didn't know what to do with it.

Cora took pity on him. Someone should have taught this man some social graces.

"Mrs. Hudson liked her book," she said, trying to start a conversation.

Simon looked up from the dilemma he held in his hand. "She opened it?"

"Yes, she said there was no need to wait until the party, since you weren't going to be there."

He nodded and looked down at the present again. He wiggled it just enough to make the curls bob.

"You can open it now," she suggested.

"What did you get in the gift exchange?"

"A plastic moose-head pencil holder for my desk."

His head jerked up, and he looked her in the eye. "Really?"

She affirmed her sincerity with a very serious nod of the head.

He grinned.

She grinned back.

She giggled.

He laughed. "That has to be the worst office-party gift I've ever heard of."

Now she felt nerves pulling her in two directions. Simon the Sour Boss was going to hate a lighthearted gift. Why had she succumbed to silliness? But the man needed to lighten up. Her gift was perfect.

She pointed to the present in his hand. "That might top it."

He pulled the ribbons off and tucked them in his coat pocket. The paper came off next, and he chortled at the picture on the box. "Is this what it really is, or did you reuse the box?"

"That's really it." She held her breath.

Simon slit the clear plastic wrapping with a thumbnail and opened the box. He pulled out the contents. A miniature desk calendar with no Mondays. An extremely small pad of paper marked *Suggestions*. A tiny box for the suggestions that had the slot duct-taped shut. A sign that said, *Out*. Flipped over, it still said, *Out*. All together the desk set contained ten tiny, absurd items that mocked traditional office paraphernalia.

A streetlamp illuminated his face, and she saw his winsome smile. The smile changed him from nicely handsome to incredibly attractive. His lips twitched. "Thank you, Miss Crowden. Your gift is much appreciated."

"You're welcome. It's Crowder."

He nodded again, still smiling. Cora found herself smiling too. Mr. Derrick should release that blast of charm more often. The girls in the office would find it breathtaking. She shook herself back to reality and headed for her money pit of a car.

Mr. Derrick made sure she was locked in before he returned to his vehicle.

She cracked her window. "Merry Christmas, and thanks for the lift," she said as he opened the driver's door. The tangle of ribbon curls from the package stuck out of his tailored black overcoat. Their bright, bouncy colors looked ludicrous in the dark night.

He lifted a hand in a farewell gesture, then he said good-bye instead of grunting, as he had in the bookstore.

One nice notch up from nothing. Cora acknowledged the polite exchange as she nosed her car out onto the street. Then a happy zing shot down her previous opinion of her boss's boss. She would have to revise her opinion of Mr. Derrick. Who would have thought that under solemn, silent, and serious was a personality?

Turning her mind to more practical matters, Cora reached out and punched the heat control on the dashboard. She hit the Defrost button next, throwing the warm air onto the windshield. She shut the heater off and waited for the engine to warm up. Past time to go home.

She mulled over the chores she wanted to get done this weekend. Then her thoughts turned to what she could still get done this evening.

Find the cat. Where was Skippy hiding this morning? She'd obviously found a new spot. Cora puzzled over the oddity. But the problem would solve itself soon. She'd ferret Skippy out. That cat had no way to escape, and how hard could it be to find one fat cat in a one-bedroom apartment?

4

Monday morning, when Cora parked her car in her slot, she recognized the car in eighty-six and knew Simon Derrick probably sat at his desk, drinking a cup of coffee and making a list. And just like Santa Claus, he would check it twice. Mr. Derrick was meticulous.

She hung her coat on a brass hook in the employee lounge and opened the locker above it. Before pushing in her purse, she removed the Wizards' Christmas Ball ticket. Irritation twitched her fingers. It had been a most unsettling weekend, from her encounter with Simon on Friday to finally finding Skippy. She closed the narrow door of her locker and leaned her head against it.

"Are you all right, Cora?" Mrs. Hudson stood behind her.

Cora took a deep breath, straightened, and smiled.

"You're sore from your accident, aren't you?"

Cora tilted her head, and the muscles in her shoulders twanged. "You know, I am." She put a hand up to gently message the nape of her neck. "You were right about it sneaking up on me."

"I bet you got all your packages off this weekend."

"I did."

"That should give you a sense of satisfaction." Mrs. Hudson's gentle expression changed to a mock scowl. "Will you change your mind and come have Christmas dinner with my family?"

Cora gave her a swift hug. "No, I have my own little tradition, and I would be out of sorts all year if I didn't get to have my own way."

"Christmas is supposed to be about people, Cora. Not rituals."

"I didn't say rituals, Mrs. Hudson. I said tradition."

The older woman tsked. "Promise me you won't be alone."

"I promise."

"Well, then get to work. We want everything caught up so the week between Christmas and New Year's won't be such a hassle while half the staff's on vacation."

"Yes ma'am." Cora saluted, but she didn't go straight to her desk.

She made a detour down the middle aisle and knocked softly on Mr. Derrick's door. Of course, she could see him. Glass walls did not provide much privacy. He looked up and waved her in.

And he stood. Cora had noticed that he stood whenever a woman entered the room.

"Come in," he said. "What can I do for you?"

"I brought you the ticket." She handed it to him.

"Thank you. My sister will be thrilled."

"And…" Her voice trailed off.

He tilted his head, waiting.

"And it seems I can provide a kitten as well. Not by Christmas, of course, but you can bring your sister by my apartment, and she can watch how they grow."

"I thought you said your cat had no social life."

"She doesn't! I don't know how it happened." She felt tears welling up. It was silly, but all the trivial little problems of the past week welled up and overflowed. Tears ran down her cheeks.

Mr. Derrick gently pulled her into his office, closed the door, and told her to sit in the chair to the right of his desk.

"No one can see your face from there." He sat behind his desk and handed her a file. "Open it and read."

He rummaged in his bottom drawer until he found a battered box of tissues, and he placed it in her lap, under the opened file. Cora snatched at a tissue and tried to wipe her eyes without letting the whole office know she'd had a breakdown. She pressed trembling lips together. This was absurd. If she had cried in front of Mrs. Hudson, it would have been bad, but not this bad. Crying in front of your boss's boss was not recommended in any of the business courses she'd taken in college.

"I have a couple of calls to make," Mr. Derrick said. "Take a minute to get settled. But don't leave until I've given you permission."

Her head jerked up. "Permission?"

He smiled. "You'll want to wait until your face isn't blotchy anymore. I can see that, and you can't."

"Oh." She pressed the tissue to her eyes. "Thank you."

True to his word, Simon opened his planner and made his morning calls. She listened with half an ear. He used the same even tone with everyone, no false camaraderie as she heard some of the salesmen on the floor use, and no steel beneath the glove when he spoke to a man who needed a reprimand.

"Are you feeling better?"

She nodded and handed him the file. "That account should be closed. Over thirty-two percent of their merchandise has been returned or received a formal complaint."

"We're pulling the company from our placement line." He leaned back in his chair, propping his elbows on the armrests with his hands folded together. He nodded slowly. "I guess now would be a good time to tell you we did the year-end reviews last week. Your name has been put forward to cover Mrs. Hudson's position while she's on leave."

Cora jerked so violently the tissue box fell to the floor. Mr. Derrick bent over to pick it up and then put it back in his drawer. "You're surprised."

"I didn't expect this. Kelly Johnson has been here longer."

"She's not a people person. She doesn't encourage other members of the team."

"That's part of Mrs. Hudson's job?"

He smiled and shook his head. "That's not in her job description. But it makes her good at what she does."

"Do you really want me?"

An odd look passed through his eyes. She looked down at her hands. He'd probably thought she could do the job until she burst into tears over the cat. Now he must be mulling over whether she had emotional issues.

"I take recommendations and interview those who are being considered." He sighed and leaned back again. "I didn't single you out, Miss Crowden."

This time she sighed, and she outdid his sigh by a mile. "Crow-der."

He smiled, a nice smile that warmed his eyes. "I had a college roommate, Larry Crowden. He's still a great friend. I'm sorry, I can't seem to forget his name and remember yours."

All right, then he wasn't such a jerk.

He leaned forward. "I do think you're the best person for this job. We'll consider that settled. Congratulations."

She stared at him. "I didn't lose the opportunity over the cat?"

"I don't understand."

"I cried about my cat."

"Well, I figured it was probably something more than just the cat."

She shook her head in a tight little motion that made her dizzy, so she stopped. Tears threatened, and she blinked. He must think she was nuts.

"Miss Crowder, Sandy would love to see the newborn kittens. May I bring her over this week? Does Wednesday work for you?"

Zeroing in on the point. Was that his way of rescuing her from her meandering melancholy?

She nodded and stood. "I'll write out directions."

"Just give me the address, and I'll find it on the Web."

She clenched her teeth and moved to the door.

"Thank you, Mr. Derrick."

"Thank you for the ticket. And…"

"And?"

"You might want to go to the rest room and wash your face. You're still a little blotchy."

Wednesday. The boss was coming. The boss and his family.

Cora looked at her watch again. Ten after seven. Simon Derrick had said seven fifteen. He'd called and said everyone but Granddad wanted to see the kittens. Did she mind?

She said she didn't, but her apartment was a carefully designed place of refuge, and she was being invaded. First by immaculately conceived kitties, and now by a man from the office and his family. Did she mind? Yes, she did.

She was so nervous she couldn't eat, but she could certainly tidy. She whizzed around like the Queen of England would be knocking at her door.

She checked on Skippy and her kitties. The calico had tolerated her all weekend, for the most part, but she had moved her kittens to a new hiding place whenever Cora got too intrusive. It had taken until midweek for Cora and Mama Skippy to come to an understanding about the precious kitties. And now outsiders threatened their calm.

She jumped when the doorbell rang. Biting her lip, she hastened to open it, forgetting to look through the peephole.

They stood in a bunch, three women, and Simon Derrick behind them. There was no little girl. Then the roundest and youngest lady blinked behind impossibly pink glasses, and Cora understood.

She smiled and reached out to take her hand. "You must be Sandy. Please, everyone, come in."

After the introductions, Cora led them on tiptoe to the hall closet. It had double doors that opened from the center, and Skippy had learned to open them the first day she came to the apartment.

One half held shelves for linens and storage, and the other had a rod for coats and sweaters on hangers.

Cora whispered, "I think she's in here now. She keeps moving her babies."

Sandy sidled as close to Cora as she could and peered at the slatted closet door. She whispered back, even quieter than Cora. "Why?"

"I guess Skippy thinks I'm too nosy."

She eased open the door and heard three feminine "ahs" behind her. Five little kittens snuggled along Skippy's stomach, attached and nursing. Mama cat lifted her head and said, "Yee-ow!" She narrowed her eyes and gave the intruders a glare.

Simon's sister reached for a kitten, but her mother caught her arm. "Not yet, Sandy. They're too little."

One kitty let go and fell away from its mommy. It lay on its back, not moving.

Sandy gasped. "Is it okay?"

Cora put an arm around the young lady's back. "Yes, she's fine."

"Passed out," said Aunt Mae. "Drunk on milk."

Sandy leaned farther into the closet. "Why aren't they cute?"

Cora laughed. "They'll look better in a few days. Their hair will fill out, and in two weeks or so, they'll open their eyes."

"There are five kittens." She turned serious eyes to Cora. "Which one is mine?"

"You can choose," Cora said, "but we have to wait for six to eight weeks before they can leave their mother."

She nodded. "Okay." Sandy peered at the kittens, looking from one to the next. "I can't decide."

"There will be plenty of time for you to make a decision," Cora said.

Sandy lifted a bag she'd been carrying and handed it to Cora. "These are for you. I baked them with Granddad."

Cora peeked inside and smelled chocolate before she even caught sight of the cookies. "Chocolate chip?"

Sandy nodded. "Do you like chocolate chip? It's the only kind of cookies Granddad will make."

"I love chocolate chip, and I have some hot cocoa mix. Come into the living room, and we'll have a party."

Sandy gazed longingly into the linen cupboard.

Cora gave her a little hug. "You can come back and see them before you leave. When they're bigger, Skippy will let us hold them."

Simon still hung in the background. She gestured toward the living room, and he chose a chair in the corner, while all the women crowded into the kitchen. Cora had more help than she needed to get the cocoa started. The milk, she was told, had to go in a saucepan and couldn't be microwaved. Aunt Mae asked if Cora had any cinnamon. Mrs. Derrick put the mugs in hot water to warm them.

At first Cora thought she would get claustrophobic with so

many bodies in her tiny kitchen, but the three ladies were fun to be with, chatting and helping one another, and even bursting into song. Christmas songs, of course. Cora peeked around the door frame and saw Simon sitting under the reading lamp with a Max Lucado book from her bookcase.

Since Cora had no natural cocoa powder or even carob, the brand-name powdered mix would have to do. Aunt Mae was nice about it but insisted that Cora shop at the natural-food grocery and gave her instructions about what to buy. After ten minutes of careful stirring, the cocoa steamed but wasn't allowed to boil.

When they brought mugs and a plate of cookies to the living room, Simon took his cup and a cookie but went right back to the book. The women took care of the conversation. Before long, Cora found herself unloading her feelings about her cat.

"I just don't understand how it happened. I tried so hard to keep her safe and protected. But somehow she got out anyway. It almost feels like I've been betrayed." To her horror, Cora felt the tears well up again.

"Oh my." Simon's mother put her hand on Cora's shoulder. "Why is this so troubling?"

Cora sniffed. "How did Skippy get pregnant? She never leaves the apartment."

"Has she spent the night at the vet's recently?" asked Aunt Mae.

"I thought of that." Cora sighed. "She spent a day there, but it was six months ago."

Mrs. Derrick sipped her cocoa. "Does anyone else go in and out of your apartment to do cleaning or maintenance? Someone could have let your cat out."

"The apartment complex has inspections and a maintenance man. I suppose that could be a possibility. But no one reported she got out."

"They probably assumed, because they found her and managed to get her home, that it didn't matter."

Cora sniffed. "Yes, you're probably right."

Aunt Mae patted her shoulder. "But that doesn't explain why you find it so upsetting."

Cora glanced around the concerned faces of the three women. Simon had his nose in the book, apparently oblivious to the female chatter.

"When I was growing up," she confided, "my sister was three years younger than me." She stopped, and Mrs. Derrick nodded, encouraging her to go on. "Because of the situation at home, I basically raised her."

Cora tried to think of a way to get out of telling this story. But now that she'd started, there didn't seem to be a graceful way to stop. These ladies were so sympathetic and calm. Still, she never told this story. Never. She looked from Simon's mother's eyes to his aunt's serene expression. Mrs. Derrick rubbed a soft circle on her back. Their peace reassured Cora. The sob that had almost escaped eased away in a relieved sigh. Cora crossed her legs, pressing one against the other. "When she was thirteen, she began sneaking out. By the time she was fourteen, she was pregnant. I didn't know she had been sneaking out."

Mrs. Derrick nodded ever so slightly. "So you felt it was your fault."

Cora shrugged. "Some, but the worst of it was nobody but me thought it was horrible. My sister laughed over my being shocked and upset. And"—Cora made a face—"she told me to butt out of her life." She gave a half laugh. "I guess I'm expecting Skippy to tell me to get out of her life."

Sandy reached across and patted Cora's knee. "She won't do that," she said seriously. "She's a cat."

Cora blinked rapidly, suppressing her tears and trying to keep a straight face at the same time. The others broke into laughter.

Aunt Mae slapped her knee. "Leave it to Sandy to bring out the most important point." She turned to Cora. "Cats are less complicated than people. They're less likely to betray you."

Mrs. Derrick nodded. "People are born with the ability to hurt one another. Without Jesus, they're just bound to. Just think how often we, who have the benefit of the Holy Spirit, manage to mess things up."

Cora felt her mouth drop open. "You're Christians?"

"Yes," said Aunt Mae. "All of us." She nodded to each of the family.

"Even Simon," said Sandy. "Granddad says it's harder for a man to be a Christian."

"Really?" Cora turned to look at the man who was supposedly mesmerized by Max Lucado's wisdom. His ears were pink. "Why is it harder for a man?"

"Stubborn and proud, is what I'd say," offered Aunt Mae. "Men get double doses of both at birth."

Mrs. Derrick shook her head. "No, I think it's because they're too busy to sit and worship."

"I'm plenty busy," said Aunt Mae.

Cora turned to Sandy. "What does Granddad say is the reason?"

Sandy recited, "It takes a man a while to get his head around the fact that"—she pinched her lips in thought, then nodded—"love makes you stronger, not weaker." She turned to her big brother. "Is that right, Simon?"

"Yes, that's right."

5

A shadow fell across Cora's office desk. She looked up and saw Sandy standing beside her.

"I came on the bus," Sandy said. "We're going to look for a costume. Simon says he couldn't find Sage Street. Do you know where it is?"

"Yes, I do." Cora pushed a lock of hair back from her face and tucked it behind her ear. "I don't think I've ever seen you in the office before."

"Simon sometimes brings me on Saturdays. But I rode the bus today. I'm very good at riding the bus."

"I'm glad to see you, and guess what? I have pictures of the kitties."

Sandy's eyes opened wide, and a smile tilted her lips.

Cora tapped a few commands on her keyboard, and Skippy appeared with her babies.

"Aww!" Sandy dropped to her knees beside the desk chair to get a better view.

Cora clicked through the ten pictures she'd taken before leaving for work. "They made wee little noises this morning that sounded more like squeaks than meows."

She had to go through the rotation again as three of her co-workers came up behind her to view the kittens.

Mrs. Hudson laid a hand on Sandy's shoulder. "Is this a friend of yours, Cora?"

Sandy got up as Cora said, "Yes, Sandy is my friend."

Simon's sister reached a hand out to shake Mrs. Hudson's hand. "I am Cora's friend. And I'm Simon's sister. My name is Sandy."

Mrs. Hudson took her plump hand, shook it, but held on. "Did you come to have lunch with Simon?"

Sandy nodded so hard she had to push her glasses back up her nose. "And we're going to go shopping. We're going to a Christmas ball, and I need a gown."

Mrs. Hudson looked suitably impressed.

"We're going to walk to Sage Street and go to a costume shop.

But Simon said he couldn't find Sage Street. Do you know where it is?"

Now Mrs. Hudson looked puzzled.

"You don't know where it is either?" Sandy's expression crumpled a bit. "What if we can't find it? That would be awful."

"No Sandy, I was wondering what kind of ball it is and if you need a prom-dress-type gown or a costume."

Sandy beamed. "I can have anything I want. It's a wizards' ball. It's magical. I can wear a dress like a princess or a fairy or Little Bo Peep. And Simon said one of the shops on Sage Street is a costume shop."

"Sponsors?" Mrs. Hudson looked to Cora for an explanation.

She shrugged. "I can't tell you much more. The Web site has a list of stores that promote the ball. Probably for the free advertisement. And the pictures of balls from previous years show all sorts of costumes, gowns, whatever. And, of course, since it's a wizards' ball, there are people dressed in wizard costumes. It looks like fun."

Sandy took Cora's hand. "Will you go with us?"

"To the ball?" Cora shook her head. Going to the dance with Sandy would be going to the dance with Mr. Derrick. That would be beyond uncomfortable, though for one teeny-tiny bit of a very short second, the thought of dating her boss's boss felt like it could be *made* to be comfortable.

Sandy was tapping Cora on the shoulder. "To Sage Street. You know where it is, right?"

"Your brother has been there. It really isn't hard to find. And I have to work."

"We're going at lunchtime. Simon will say it's all right."

Through a space in the crowd around Cora's desk, Cora glimpsed Simon coming their way. She tipped her head toward him, and the office girls took the hint, dispersing to attend to business. That left Sandy and Mrs. Hudson to greet Mr. Derrick.

He hugged his sister. "And what is it Simon says is all right?"

Sandy grinned at Cora. "That's a joke. We try to make sentences come out to say 'Simon says' because it's a game." She turned back to her big brother. "Can Cora come to help you find the street?"

Simon glanced around the room. Cora followed his gaze. Several employees hustled to make themselves look busy. Simon's eyes came back to the three women at Cora's desk.

Mrs. Hudson leaned toward him. "It's not going to start office gossip for the two of you to take your sister out to lunch and do a little shopping. I'll cover Cora's calls until she gets back, so you don't have to hurry Sandy."

Simon hesitated for a moment. Cora wondered why it was so hard for him to go out to lunch with her. Many of the employees invaded the nearby eateries in flocks.

Finally, he cleared his throat. "All right, then. Are you ready for lunch, Miss Crow-der?"

"Almost. I should send off a couple of e-mails before we go. It won't take long. They're already written." Cora turned back to her monitor as Mrs. Hudson and Mr. Derrick walked away.

She let a little smile escape.

She suppressed a giggle.

She told herself to get a grip.

A romantic Serious Simon didn't jive with anything she knew about the man. And she wasn't all that good at relationships.

Sandy stood at Cora's shoulder and watched the kitten pictures disappear. Cora's e-mail program popped onto the screen.

Sandy sighed. "I saw you on Simon's computer at home."

What? My picture on his computer? She looked up at Sandy, and her shock must have registered on her face, because the young woman took a step back.

Sandy turned red. "That's okay, isn't it? We saw you when Simon showed me the Wizards' Christmas Ball Web site. Simon said it was just a shadow. But I think it was you."

"Oh, I saw a face on that site too. It must be something wrong with their program."

"Did you see a lady too?" asked Sandy.

No. She hadn't seen a lady. She'd seen a man. And, well, as crazy as it seemed, the man looked a lot like Simon Derrick. That had to be just the power of suggestion. She hadn't thought it looked like anyone until Sandy brought up this whole absurd idea. It wasn't her on his screen, and it wasn't him on her screen.

"Cora." Sandy's soft voice made Cora jump. "Did you see a lady?"

"No. It was a man, but just a blink of an image, nothing you could focus on." She put her hands back on her keyboard and scrutinized the office PC—the good old reliable office PC that she could look at all day long and not see a handsome man in his T-shirt with a shadow of beard darkening his chin. "Give me a minute, Sandy, and I'll be ready to go."

She found the e-mail addresses and put them in the To box, attached the documents, wrote a quick closing, and hit Send.

She stood. "Let's go get my coat and purse. I'll show you where the employees take coffee breaks."

They passed Simon discussing something with Mrs. Hudson at her desk. Cora nodded at Simon as they made eye contact. "We're almost ready."

By the time she and Sandy returned, Simon waited for them by the elevator.

"Are you sure you want to walk, Candy-Sandy?" he asked. "We might get lost, and then it'll be a long haul."

"I can do it." She laughed. "And besides, I know you. If we walk too long, you'll stick me in a taxi, and I like taxi rides."

"Well, we're not going to get lost. I put the address in a map search, and it took a few tries, but Sage Street popped up on a special program without any trouble. It didn't come up on the usual program I use but redirected to another search site. Sage Street is where Miss Crowder and I left it last week."

The bell dinged, and the elevator door slid open. They waited for it to empty, then stepped in. Sandy stood next to the control panel. "Three passengers got off, and three passengers got on." When the door shut, she asked, "Simon says what number?"

"SL will put us on street level."

She punched the lettered button. "Good, I want to see the store decorations up close."

Simon made a mournful face. "I can only be gone two hours, Sandy, or I'll have to stay more than an extra hour tonight."

Sandy turned to Cora. "Will you have to work an extra hour tonight too?"

"I'm not planning to stay with you the whole two hours," Cora said. "I'll help you find the street, then eat lunch. But I really need to get back."

Simon chucked Sandy under her chin. "I talked to Cora's boss, and she has permission to stay out for an extended lunch, and she will not have to stay an hour to make up for it."

Cora's eyes widened.

"Mrs. Hudson gave you as long as it takes." One corner of

Simon's mouth tilted upward. "She said you volunteered to work next week when so many others will be on vacation. She also said you had volunteered every Christmas since you first came to Sorenby's."

Sandy bounced on her toes and skipped out as soon as the elevator door opened. "Which way?" Her head swung back and forth.

Simon pulled Cora's arm through his and led her up to where his sister had stopped in the lobby. Cora started to pull away, but then he tucked his other arm through Sandy's. "This way," he said and started them toward the Twiller Street exit.

Cora left her arm resting in the gentleman's care and puzzled over the vagaries of social etiquette. She didn't believe any man had ever escorted her like this. Mixed feelings kept her back stiff. The closeness felt odd and comforting at the same time. The pressure of his arm unsettled her but also gave her confidence. She wavered between accepting the pleasant associations of being on the arm of an attractive man and the fact that she had no right to claim any relationship with Mr. Derrick.

But he'd made the gesture, and he didn't seem to think anything of it. Why should she be so concerned? She searched the faces of people passing on the sidewalk. No one else seemed to think Cora Crowder walking down the street on the arm of Simon Derrick was strange.

Simon stood with his hands in his pockets as Cora and Sandy ogled the costumes in the window of the shop. Velvet-covered mannequins modeled the gowns, and a slumbering cat lay curled on a plush brocade pillow in a basket inside the display window.

They'd walked the distance in less than ten minutes, made no wrong turns, and found the street just as easily as he had the day he visited the bookstore. Sandy's rosy cheeks and the puff of vapor from her breath reminded him that she needed to be hustled out of the chill wind.

"I thought the idea of shopping was to go into the store," he said.

Sandy laughed, but Cora tossed him a look that said she didn't know whether he was joking or upset. He smiled in an effort to clear up her confusion. She returned his smile, and he opened the door. Bells hanging at the top of the door frame rang, and he gestured for the ladies to enter.

A muffled voice came from among the many racks of clothing. "Was that the bells, Bonnie?"

"I think it was."

Two of the collections of long gowns jiggled and swayed. Simon expected the women embodying the voices to appear through the small gaps between racks. Instead, two old ladies appeared from under the racks of dresses and peered up.

"May we help you?" said the one on the right. "Are you going to the ball?"

"Yes!" said Sandy. "You have cats?"

"Cats?" Simon looked quizzically at his sister.

Sandy grinned and pointed to various spots in the room. Three felines in addition to the one they'd seen in the window seemed to be residents of the store.

"What are their names?" Sandy pulled off her gloves and inched toward the closest tabby. "I'm going to get a kitten, and I have to think of good names for cats. Do they like to be petted?"

"Well," said the shopkeeper, crawling out from the left side of the racks, "we have Muffin, Cupcake, Marmalade, and Twinkie."

"Marmalade didn't come with the others," explained the other woman. "He would have been Toast or, perhaps, French Toast. Yes, you can pet them."

Sandy nodded and stroked the cat's side. "Which one is this?"

"Muffin."

"Do you ladies need some help getting to your feet?" asked Simon.

"Oh, how kind," said one.

"But unnecessary," said the other.

"Just turn your head," said the first.

"We aren't as graceful as we used to be."

Simon, Cora, and Sandy turned toward the door. Behind them, two grunts and a whooshing sound accompanied a brisk stir of the air in the shop. Simon almost turned to identify what had caused the sudden draft but remembered in time the old ladies' request.

"There now, you can turn back around."

"You're quick," said Sandy. "It takes Aunt Mae a lot longer to get up." She tilted her head. "And you're not even out of breath." She nodded. "You're good. What were you doing on the floor?"

"Bonnie dropped a button, and you just can't get buttons to match some of the older gowns." She came forward and took both of Sandy's hands in hers. "My name is Betty Booterbaw, and this is my sister Bonnie Booterbaw. We own the store."

"Is it fun?" asked Sandy.

"Mostly."

Sandy eyed the clothing. "I don't see any ghosts or gross costumes. Don't you do Halloween stuff?"

Simon felt the dawning of comprehension. His little sister hadn't voiced a concern but had been sending him subtle hints. Now he understood why she had insisted Miss Crowder come along. He smiled, deliberately showing that her fear didn't upset him. "Were you scared to come here, Sandy? You should have told me."

She nodded and turned big eyes to the sisters. "I don't like scary things."

Betty scowled. "You mean witches and monsters? We'd never carry that sort of costume."

"We don't believe in witches," said Bonnie. "Wizards are another thing. Old and wise, that's what the root of 'wizard' means. And did you know a wizard can be male or female?"

Betty gave her sister a frown and shook her head as if to discourage the line of conversation.

Simon stepped into the breach. "We're looking for a dress for Sandy to wear to the Wizards' Christmas Ball."

Betty Booterbaw looked around his sister to Cora. "Oh, we have lovely gowns for you, dear."

"I'm Cora, not Sandy."

Bonnie gasped. "There must be some mistake." She frowned at Simon. "You acquired a ticket to the ball, didn't you?"

Simon nodded.

Bonnie bit her lips as she turned to Cora. "And you got a ticket?"

"Yes, but I wasn't going, so I gave it to Mr. Derrick for Sandy. Do you have any dresses for Sandy?"

Simon looked at his sister's face and knew she was getting upset. What did it matter to these two old hens who went to the ball? They shouldn't make his sister feel like she wasn't good enough.

Afraid to open his mouth because indignation might make him less than tactful, he allowed Cora to handle the shopkeepers. In a minute she had a smile back on Sandy's face and the two old biddies' enthusiastic help.

"Of course." Bonnie's face broke into a smile. "I'm sure we can find something. What kind of costume are you looking for?"

His sister plunged into the racks of clothing with zeal, happily pulling out one costume after another and holding them up for his inspection. She favored fairy and princess gowns.

She picked out a few dresses, all of them pink. Besides being pink, they had another thing in common. They were all the wrong size. But Betty and Bonnie assured her they had an absolute hoard of fashions in reserve. Whatever style she picked, they would be able to find one in her size in the stockroom.

While Sandy was in the fitting room trying on a princess gown, Bonnie Booterbaw cornered Cora. "Don't you want to go to the ball?" Her face showed real concern. "I thought it was every girl's dream to attend a real ball."

She smiled and shook her head. "I haven't been to many dances. In fact, none. And, well, I wouldn't know anyone there."

Sandy's head popped out between the curtains. "You'll know us. Simon, say she can go with us."

Simon turned to Cora. This would be like taking a friend of Sandy's. That's all. This wasn't even as hard as asking a girl out in high school or college. Back then his hands shook, his voice trembled, and the invitation stumbled off his tongue. He was a real nerd.

He cleared his throat and shoved his hand in his coat pocket. "Miss Crowd—er, Sandy and I would be honored if you would accompany us to the Wizards' Christmas Ball."

"That's all fine and dandy," said Betty Booterbaw, "but she doesn't have a ticket."

"You're listed as a sponsor," said Simon. "Don't you sell tickets?"

Both Booterbaw sisters shook their heads. Bonnie looked at

Betty. Betty shrugged her shoulders. Bonnie sighed. "Don't have even one left."

Cora put a hand on his arm. "It's all right, Mr. Derrick. Really, it is."

One of the cats stood and stretched and started a yowly conversation with another.

"Oh dear," said Bonnie and covered her ears.

"What's wrong?" asked Sandy's plaintive voice from the changing cubicle.

"Nothing that can be explained." Betty scooped up the two cats and dumped them out the front door, bells ringing wildly.

Bonnie put another out, but while the door was open, one of the cats outside slinked in. Simon and Cora tried to help, but one cat out always meant one or two back in. This process went on for five full minutes, before a giggle made them all stop and turn.

Sandy stood outside the fitting room in a gown meant for a princess. She held a small satin clutch purse in her hand.

Simon stared. *Transformed.* That was the word he wanted. His unsophisticated little sister looked enchanting.

She grinned at all of them, and the cats quit their caterwauling.

Sandy twirled around almost gracefully. She patted her full skirt down a bit, then turned expectant eyes on her big brother. "How are we going to get Cora a ticket?"

6

Cora felt terrible. Sandy was not going to enjoy the ball with her brother because she had it in her head that Cora ought to go too. But Cora didn't want to go. Simon Derrick had practically been forced to issue the politely worded invitation. If Sandy had not been standing right there, Simon would have dodged the circumstance neatly. And besides that, at this point, Cora couldn't go. No ticket provided a perfect excuse.

Betty Booterbaw clapped her hands together. "I know. We'll call Billy Wizbotterdad."

Cora blinked. "From the bookstore?"

"Not really. He's Bill's son. Doesn't work at the shop. He's a whiz at computers."

For some reason Betty's statement set Bonnie off in a fit of giggles.

"What good will it do to call this Billy?" asked Simon.

"Oh, he organizes the ticket part of the ball, among other things." Betty shushed Bonnie, then turned back to their customers. "He'll know if any of the shops still have tickets left, or if anyone has returned a ticket."

She clapped her hands together once more. "There! We have a plan. Bonnie, help Sandy out of the dress. Is that the one you want, dear? You look lovely."

Smiling broadly, Sandy nodded as Bonnie bustled her back to the fitting room.

"Um," said Simon, "I think I better look at the price."

Betty's words were muffled as she bent behind a counter. "Ninety-nine dollars and ninety-nine cents."

She pulled out a battered black phone directory, opened it, and flipped through the pages.

"Here he is." Betty picked up a telephone, the old-fashioned kind that had a horn-shaped base that held the mouthpiece on the top. A bracket cradled an earpiece on the side. She lifted the earpiece and jiggled the bracket. "Hello, June, get me Billy Wizbotterdad, please, 4893. Yes, it's about the ball. If you hear of anyone with an extra ticket, let me know." She winked at Cora and Simon. "She's putting me through."

Cora turned to Simon and pulled him toward the door. "That's impossible," she whispered, then realized even the whisper had come out too loud and lowered her voice. "That phone doesn't have a cord going to the wall."

"It's probably a cordless." He didn't sound convinced. He frowned as he stared back between racks of clothing at the old lady carrying on a lively conversation with Billy. Simon leaned closer, still watching through the gowns. "It's a mock-up of an old phone to fit the atmosphere of the shop, but it's got to be a cordless phone."

His chin almost touched the top of her head. He smelled of some wonderful aftershave. She didn't have much experience with men who smelled good. She drew in a slow, long breath, enjoying the heady fragrance.

Totally unaware of her, Simon repeated, "Cordless."

He'd broken the spell.

Cora couldn't keep the sarcasm out of her voice. "Or a cell phone."

He bent down to whisper, "No." Simon's serious tone brought her eyes to his face, now so close to her own. He stared at Betty and her contraption with a puzzled frown. "I just looked into changing my service and saw all types of cell phones. That wasn't offered by any company I researched."

"Simon!" Cora had never used his first name. Now she used it but in a tone that said, "How can you be so dense?" She gasped. What a complete ninnyhammer! Without a doubt, it was time for her to go back to work.

Simon's head turned too quickly, his nose bumping hers. They both pulled back.

"What?" he asked, his face a shade redder.

"I was being sarcastic about the cell phone."

"Oh."

This man needed lessons in the finer nuances of conversation, but Cora was not going to volunteer. She faked looking at her watch. "I've got to go. My lunch hour is over."

Simon grabbed her arm. "No, you don't."

"No?"

"Remember?" He spoke in a rush. "You have Mrs. Hudson's permission."

He clamped his mouth shut. An uncomfortable moment stretched. Cora wondered if she should pull her arm out of his grasp or just wait.

Simon let out a sigh and spoke in a slow, controlled manner. "And we haven't had lunch." He looked toward the fitting rooms. "And this gown business is way over my head."

Cora agreed with that assessment. Sandy was going to need some intimate apparel suitable for under the dress, and she'd give a monkey's banana her brother hadn't even thought of that. Perhaps his mother would take charge in that department.

Bonnie brought out Sandy's dress on a padded hanger and hung it on a hook behind the counter. "We'll steam press this before we bag it so it will be nice and fresh for the young lady."

Cora's attention shifted from the gown to the two old ladies and then to a cat stretched out on a glass case filled with hats. She whispered to Simon, "All of this is strange. Even the price of the dress is wrong."

"Too much?" asked Simon.

Cora rolled her eyes. "About six hundred dollars too little."

Simon shook his head in disbelief. "Well, Betty did say it was an old dress."

"Tack on another hundred or two for the word 'antique.' "

Betty laughed into the mouthpiece of whatever it was she held. "Thanks, Billy. I'll send the customers by the candy shop."

She hung up and waved Simon and Cora to come back to the register. "I located Billy, and he said to send you to the Garland Candy Shoppe. He's having Michelle hold a ticket for you. The store's easy to find. There are ropes of candy strung in the window like Christmas garland."

Sandy came out of the back room with her coat over her arm. Her face glowed. She touched the skirt of her dress gently. "So beautiful." She tackled Simon and gave him a big hug. "Simon, I love it."

He squeezed her back. "And Betty has found another ticket. Let's go have lunch, pick up the ticket, then come back and get your dress." He smiled at the ladies behind the counter. "Do you want me to pay for it now or when we come back?"

"When you come back is fine," said Bonnie. "We'll have the dress in a nice bag, ready to carry home. Did you want the little clutch purse too?"

Sandy nodded.

"How much?" asked Simon.

"Ten dollars."

Cora poked Simon with her elbow, but he didn't seem to notice. She wanted to hiss at him but figured that would draw attention from the Booterbaw sisters. Surely Simon would get the hint. Ten dollars for that clutch was a ludicrous price. The price tag should be fifty, at least.

"Yes, we want the purse." Simon took Sandy's coat and helped her put it on.

In a minute they were back on the street among a scattered array of Christmas shoppers. Cora stewed for a moment longer as they walked, then took a deep breath of the crisp, cold air. She could smell peppermint and chocolate.

"The crowds aren't as thick here," said Simon.

Cora exhaled, enjoying the touches of Christmas spirit on the street. "That's a good thing, right?"

"Another oddity." Simon stopped in front of the glassworks

store, and Sandy became absorbed in the spun-glass ornaments and figurines.

Simon turned to Cora. "That phone is some kind of communication apparatus like a wireless intercom. Something that works only on this street so the owners can keep in communication. I bet this whole street is owned by one corporation, and it's only made to look like two rows of separate, unusual, old-fashioned shops. The whole thing is an advertising gimmick."

"There's only one thing wrong with that theory."

He squinted at her, waiting for her to speak. She caught the expectant look in his eye and realized he had focused his attention on her. Not many people really looked, really listened, really paid attention when she spoke.

"Uh." She'd forgotten what she was going to say. "Oh! Advertising. There isn't any. Hardly anyone knows about this street. No one's heard of the Wizards' Christmas Ball."

"Not no one. My pastor's heard of it."

Sandy tugged on Simon's sleeve. "I'm hungry now."

"Me too." Simon surveyed the street. A number of small carts with huge wheels and brightly colored paint dotted the street. "Where did all these vendors come from?"

Cora shoved her gloved hands into her coat pockets. The street looked like a set of a movie, or the scene could be the picture on a Christmas card. "They must come out for the lunch crowd."

"Chili!" Sandy darted to a nearby vendor where a big sign gave a menu that sounded just right for strolling down the street and window-shopping while they ate. Sandy read slowly but accurately. "Chili. Chili dogs. Chili and mac. Corn dogs. Corn on the cob. Corn pone. Simon, what's a corn pone?"

A man in a thick plaid coat with a huge white apron over it picked up a stick of corn bread with tongs. "Here ya go, little lady. This is corn pone. Give it a try."

Sandy took the offering and sank her teeth into the golden yellow stick. She turned and nodded to Simon and Cora. "It's good."

The air around the cart smelled of onions, spices, beef, and tomatoes.

Cora's stomach growled. "I'd like chili."

They joined Sandy as the man was showing her an ingenious cup divided into three deep compartments.

"My own invention," he said. "I put your chili in here, your corn pone in here, and when you get your drink from one of the other vendors, it goes right in here." He turned the molded plastic container over to reveal a thick stick handle. "You hold it here and don't get your mittens soiled."

Sandy giggled. "Like the three little kittens."

The vendor nodded seriously. "Just like the three little kittens who soiled their mittens."

Simon bought their lunch and hot apple cider from another vendor. Cora graciously accepted the treat. Who in the office would consider a vendor meal to be an intimate lunch with a higher-ranking employee? No one.

Cora smiled. She could relax and enjoy this outing. The shop, the meal, the company felt just right. Was the happiness zinging around in her heart that Christmas feeling she was trying to catch? At least she was on the scent of the real thing, right?

Carolers in old-fashioned clothing sang on the corner. One man played an accordion. The instrument fascinated Sandy, so they stood for a while, listening to older versions of traditional carols.

When the chili and corn pone disappeared, Simon collected their empty containers and tossed them in the trash barrel next to the curb. He put a ten-dollar bill in a kettle for donations and steered his ladies away from the musicians. "We need to find the candy shop."

Sandy pointed across the street. The Garland Candy Shoppe's window blinked with Christmas lights strung among festive ropes of peppermint sticks, gingerbread men, candy trains, and marsh-mallow snowmen in fake pine boughs.

They walked to the corner and crossed to the other side of the street. Sugary, spicy fragrances greeted them when Simon opened the door. White walls and ceiling dominated the showroom with alternating pale green and blue shelves that held boxes of candy. A long display case exhibited confections on white paper doilies be-hind glass. Beyond the front room, a dining area included chairs and cloth-covered round tables.

Simon leaned over and spoke quietly in Cora's ear, sending a shiver down her spine. "Looks like you can have breakfast, lunch, or dinner here. A meal of chocolate and cotton candy?"

A young woman came from the far end of the counter to greet them. "I'm Michelle. You must be the family needing one more ticket to the ball."

Cora choked, but Sandy handled the situation in her usual forthright manner. "Simon and I are family. Cora is a friend." She pulled Simon by the sleeve toward the glass case of goodies. "Can we have dessert?"

Michelle nodded to the back. "In the second room, we have a coffee and tea bar. There's a small selection of pastries at the end of this counter, near the register."

"I'm too full," said Cora.

"Really?" Sandy turned to her, her eyes big and round. "Too full for dessert?"

Simon chuckled. "I'll get you something small, Candy-Sandy, and you can take a box home to Granddad, Aunt Mae, and Mom."

Cora watched Sandy agonize, but for a surprisingly short time. She suddenly pointed at the Christmas apples, dipped half in green candy coating, half in red. Sandy chose cocoa, and Cora found a Scottish blend of tea. While Simon paid for a box of treats to take home, three drinks and the apple on a stick, she and his sister went to find a seat.

Sandy stirred her cup and blew on it. "Simon's called me

Candy-Sandy forever. That's better than Sandy-Candy. Candy-Sandy says I'm sweet. Sandy-Candy is yucky. When I was little and got too dirty, he called me that until one day I cried."

"I think all big brothers can be a little mean at times." Cora had big stepbrothers, and a little mean was not how she would describe them—but that wasn't something she'd share with Sandy.

"Simon's never mean now. He grew up." Sandy paused and, with concentrated effort, winked her right eye. "I won't grow up. It's an advantage I cherish. A gift from Jesus."

She pronounced "advantage" carefully but slurred "cherish."

Cora frowned. "What do you mean?"

"This is what Jesus said: 'Let the little children come to me, and do not hinder them, for the kingdom of God belongs to such as these. I tell you the truth, anyone who will not receive the kingdom of God like a little child will never enter it.' Then the Bible says Jesus took the children in His arms and blessed them. That means that people who think like a little child are special to God."

Cora tried to keep the surprise out of her voice. "You memorized that verse."

Sandy nodded and sipped her drink carefully. "I know lots of verses. I'm pretty good at memorizing. Better than Simon." She giggled.

"I'm not very good at that either."

"My mom helps me. Did your mom help you?"

"No, she didn't." Now that was a conversational path she did not want to follow. "Sandy, you are going to need a special slip to wear under your beautiful gown. Will your mom take you shopping for it?"

Sandy grinned and nodded. "Aunt Mae and Mom will think that's fun. And they'll make jewelry for the ball too."

Simon came to the table and deposited the festive apple in front of his sister. "There you go, Pixie."

She screwed up her face at him. "When I'm twenty-five, you have to stop calling me Pixie."

"All right. I'll remember. But you have to help think of a new nickname."

"Besides Candy-Sandy?" asked Cora.

Sandy took a bite of her apple and nodded as she chewed.

Simon sat down and handed Cora a stiff slip of paper. Cora almost groaned out loud. She held one of the elusive tickets.

"Thank you," she said instead, trying to sound delighted.

"Oh good!" Sandy's eyes crinkled behind her glasses. "Now we can go back to the nice cat ladies and pick out a dress for you."

Cora couldn't help it. The groan left her lips before she had a chance to rein it in.

Sandy put a sticky hand on Cora's sleeve. "What's the matter?"

"Oh Sandy, I've never owned a dress like those. I probably can't afford one." Considering the prices at the costume shop, she realized, that probably wasn't totally true. She threw out one more desperate and very legitimate excuse. "And I don't even know how to walk in something that big and fluffy."

Simon's sister patted her arm. "I'll help you. 'Be brave and try new things.' It's our family motto."

Cora almost reminded Sandy that she was not family and didn't have to be brave and try new things, but she looked across the table and saw Simon's quirky grin and uplifted eyebrows. All right. Just this once, she'd "be brave and try new things."

7

Stubborn.

And a fast talker.

Cora Crowder had his goat. And probably his cow and chickens as well. He couldn't remember all the reasons she'd given for why she couldn't shop for a dress at the store then and there.

Simon finally hustled Sandy and Miss Crowder out of the Booterbaw Costume Shoppe and down Sage Street so that Sandy could catch her bus back home. Encumbered by the package containing the pink princess costume, he let Sandy and Cora chatter as they walked. He took the job of transporting the prized dress quite seriously. And he didn't mind the opportunity to eavesdrop.

Cora listened to Sandy, really listened. Few people outside the family did. This was one of the preconceived ideas that drove him crazy. Some people took one look at his sister and decided she wouldn't have much to say, but in actuality, Sandy was quite a thinker, almost a philosopher in her straight manner of looking at things.

Cora laughed with Sandy, and as she did, Sandy came out of her shell and said some pretty outrageous things. Cora took it all in stride. The two stopped to look in a window, and both young women glowed as they gazed at the display of tiny houses. Sandy looked like an elf. Cora looked like…an angel. His heart warmed just to see the joy in her expression. He cut the feeling short. He needed to appreciate the lady for her kindness to his sister and her efficiency at work. He didn't need to go overboard and wonder how it would feel to pull her into his arms and kiss her.

Cora Crowder. She made Sandy smile, but she gave him acid indigestion. Though to be fair, maybe the chili caused the burn in his esophagus.

Why couldn't she just relax, commit to going to the ball, go back to the store, and choose a dress? She had said she had to pray about it. Was that just an excuse, or was the woman really going to go home, read her Bible, and pray about whether to go with him to the ball?

If his arms weren't laden with this huge cloth bag containing yards and yards of satin and gauze, he'd kick himself. What right did he have to mock this woman's desire to ask God for direction? Praying was something he did, but he didn't talk about it. And if he prayed about going to a dance, it would be one of those quick "this is what's going on" prayers. Who needed heavenly guidance over whether or not to accompany a nice man and his little sister to a ball? Maybe Cora Crowder didn't consider Simon Derrick a nice man.

Simon stewed, and the girls talked.

At the bus stop, Simon reassured Sandy that Cora would indeed get a dress and go to the ball, all the time casting sideways glances at the noncommittal Cora. After they said good-bye and put his little sister on a bus home, he and Miss Crowder walked in silence to their office building. She thanked him for lunch and stepped into the elevator going up. He took the next elevator going down.

He stashed Sandy's dress in the trunk of his car and stood for a moment, looking at the car in slot eighty-eight.

On the cement wall between their two cars, someone had fastened a poster. The colorful glossy print looked very much like the front page of the Wizards' Christmas Ball Web site. *What an odd place for an ad.* He chuckled. The genius who designed this ad had again left off the purchase information for the tickets. Simon returned to the bank of elevators, wondering who else would come to this crazy dance.

He walked to the elevator. He hoped Cora decided to come. If she didn't, Sandy would be disappointed. Simon rode up alone. He looked at himself in the mirrored elevator walls. He straightened his tie, smoothed down his hair, and checked his teeth for vestiges of chili. He caught his own gaze in the reflection.

If Cora didn't come, he'd be disappointed. Now that was something he hadn't planned on.

Hours later, Simon sorted the files on his desk into piles. He glanced up, through his glass walls, and down the aisle framed by the sales-team cubicles. A few employees still wandered the office pool, probably those who would take off time between Christmas and New Year's. No one wanted to come back to a desk with overdue work, so they tried to get ahead.

Cora Crowder passed into and out of his narrow corridor of vision. She had a strong work ethic. She had had a long lunch, and she was going to make up the time. Mrs. Hudson had told her to go home. He'd told her to go home. She didn't.

Stubborn woman.

She glided through the half light of the after-hours office. She turned to look down the middle aisle directly at him. The instinct to avoid eye contact fled. Seeing her at the end of a tiring day actually lifted his spirits. Cora Crowder was kind, attractive, sweet. No, Cora wasn't sweet. Sandy was sweet. Cora had something deeper than sweet. She blinked, and Simon realized he'd been staring. He smiled. She turned quickly away, and the moment lost its hold on him. Somehow Cora didn't bring out as much awkwardness in him as did the women he'd tried to date in the past. He didn't feel like he'd had a close call, a narrow escape. Like any minute he would make a fool of himself.

He flipped his pencil through his fingers and tapped the eraser on his desk. Flipped it again and tapped the lead tip. Pursuit. That's what he wanted, not flight. He grinned and returned to putting his desk in order.

Cora pushed the GL button in the elevator and leaned back against the mirrored wall as the door swooshed shut. She closed her eyes and allowed the vibration of the moving car to soothe her shoulder muscles. She had finished all of today's work, and the clock said 6:45. When she'd seen her full in-box after the long lunch, her heart had nearly stopped. How could the thing overflow when she'd only been gone two hours and twenty minutes?

The extra hours this evening hadn't been too bad. Several co-workers also worked late. Jeff Stockton pulled out his CD player, and they listened to some modern renditions of old Christmas favorites. And Simon had been in his glass office.

The elevator bell dinged, and the door slid open. Pushing away from the wall, Cora reached into her bag for her keys. Once she had them tight in her right hand with one protruding from her fist to gouge an attacker, she stepped into the well-lit garage. She rounded a corner, keeping alert as they had taught her in the defense course she took, and squeezed her eyes shut. She opened them and shook her head. The car tilted. The money pit had a flat tire.

Her eyes narrowed, and she looked around suspiciously. Disabling the car was one of the ploys the instructor had listed. She looked at the sign right by her head. "Security 24/7." Supposedly, no one could drive into this lot without a pass card. But what about walking in? Turning around to head back to get one of the men to lend a hand would be a smart move. The elevator dinged. She heard the door open and then Simon Derrick's voice.

"No, I'm just now leaving the office, but Sandy couldn't have made it to her Bible study tonight anyway. No need to send someone to give her a ride." Pause. "Thanks, Spence, but I talked to Mom, and she's already gone to bed." Pause. "I'll tell you about it tomorrow."

Simon rounded the corner, and Cora jumped out of his way. "Oh!" He looked from her to her car and back again. "Looks like I'm going to change a flat tire," he said into the phone. Pause. "Have you ever tried to change a tire in a suit of shining armor?" He laughed, said "Good night," and flipped his cell phone shut.

Cora relaxed. The cavalry had arrived. No, wrong era. The knight had come to rescue the fair maiden's trusty steed. Simon smiled, eyes crinkling, and his gaze connected with hers. She smiled back, just enjoying looking at him. Then, as if someone popped a bubble, they both started and looked away.

"Um"—Cora pointed to her car in a halfhearted gesture—"I can change a tire, I think."

He looked back at her with his eyebrows raised.

"We had to change one when I took a driver's ed course."

He was smiling again.

She grinned back. "I'd much rather help someone than do it all by myself."

Simon bowed. "I volunteer for the role of someone."

"Thanks."

Cora handed him her keys, and he opened the trunk. "Ah, an old blanket."

"In case I'm caught in a blizzard."

"And a spare tire." He pushed the covering of the bottom of the trunk aside. "And the jack. May I use the blanket to protect my clothes?"

"Of course."

Cora watched as he took off his overcoat and suit jacket and rolled up his sleeves. He didn't talk. But it was a comfortable non-talking. He opened the driver's door, sat down, and did something.

"What did you do?" she asked.

"Made sure the car was in park and set the emergency brake."

"Oh."

He looked around in her trunk again. What did he need besides the tire and the jack thing?

"What are you looking for now?"

"An air-pressure gauge. Do you have one?"

"Umm…"

"I'll take that as a no." He went to his car and opened the trunk. Sandy's dress-in-a-bag took up the entire space, but he reached to one side and pulled out the right tool in one try. He checked the pressure on Cora's spare. "Okay. We're good to go."

He pulled a brick out of his trunk and went around to the front of the car, where he wedged it against a tire.

"You carry bricks in your trunk?"

"Helps with traction. I carry a couple of bags of sand too. We have some hills in our neighborhood that don't always get plowed."

He popped the hubcap off with the tire iron in one sure motion. She liked the way his hands worked the lug wrench. Muscles rippled under his shirt across his shoulders.

Oh my! Cora looked around the garage. She needed a distraction.

Only a half-dozen cars still sat in their slots, and that included hers and Simon's. She glanced at her watch. Seven.

Skippy would be hungry. Cora looked down as Simon placed the jack under her car. He lay down on the blanket and firmly gripped the jack and gave it a little tug. He straightened and began to pump the jack handle.

"I'm so glad you're doing this." Cora blushed when he looked up at her. "I think I probably would have dropped the car on my foot or something."

He winked at her. "We aren't done yet. Maybe I'll drop the car."

"Don't you dare!"

He laughed and went back to work. He finished removing the

flat and put on the spare with no difficulty. Cora studied the diagram on the inside of her trunk lid and decided she would have spent a great deal of time with her head twisted sideways to read the directions and not much time with the tire before she would have given up. But Simon seemed to have practice in this area. Or maybe men just came with a chromosome that made it easy to change a tire. With the jack locked in place and the blanket refolded and put away, Simon closed the trunk.

He nodded and said, "That'll do, Pig."

"What?"

"It's from a movie Sandy likes. Well, in truth, we all like the story." He picked up his overcoat from the backseat of his car and shrugged into it.

"I don't think I've seen it."

Simon gazed past her. "It's gone."

"The movie?"

"No, the poster."

Cora looked at the wall where Simon stared. "I don't think anyone's allowed to put posters down here."

"Yeah, I think you're right, but there was a Wizards' Christmas Ball poster down here earlier."

Cora lifted her eyebrows. "Really? The ball that has no advertisements had a poster right between our two cars?"

Simon shook his head, a look of amused bewilderment on his face. "They still didn't have any information about where to get tickets, how much they cost, and come to think of it, where the ball will be held."

"They seem to be a rather flighty bunch of organizers."

"If I hadn't seen pictures of past balls on their Web site, I wouldn't be taking Sandy."

Cora waited. Simon buttoned his coat and rummaged through his pockets for his keys.

"They're on your dash," she said. "You left them there after you opened your trunk to get the air-pressure gauge."

"Ah! Thanks. Well, I'll see you tomorrow morning."

"Thank you." She fingered her keys as she circled her car. "I appreciate your help."

"You're welcome." He got in his car as she got in hers.

His engine roared to life, but he waited a moment for her to turn the key in her car. Then he waved and backed out.

After he had driven away, Cora shoved her gearshift into reverse.

And that's another reason why I don't want to go to a romantic ball with you, Mr. Simon Derrick. Sandy wants me to go, and I think it would be fun to spend the evening with her and you, big brother. But you, big brother, are clueless. You could have said, "If I hadn't seen pictures of past balls on their Web site, I wouldn't be taking Sandy and you."

Cora continued to fume as she approached the street.

But he couldn't say that. He couldn't because he didn't think of it. He didn't think of it because I'm not the one he's interested in taking.

He's not interested in taking me to the ball, because for him it's not about romance and dinner and dancing and your destiny. It's about giving his sister a delightful time and a good memory to cherish. And that's a good and noble thing, right? I don't need to be so hurt.

It's not all about me. It should be about Sandy.

Snowflakes fell on her windshield as she nosed out of the underground parking.

"And I don't begrudge Sandy that," Cora said as she waited for a light to turn from red to green. "But I want more for me than a haphazard, 'Oh sure, she can go along too.'"

The light changed, two straggling pedestrians scurried out of the road, and Cora stepped lightly on the gas. Her cell phone played the opening notes of Beethoven's fifth symphony. "Duh duh duh duhhh." Her mother.

She liberated the phone from her purse and flipped it open, keying the speakerphone button. She laid the phone on the console next to her seat.

"Hi, Mom."

"Your sister Guinevere is going to Jamaica for the holidays."

"That sounds...sunny."

"Aren't you going to ask who's taking her?"

Cora grimaced as she turned right onto a more crowded street. "Who's taking her?"

"Bobby!"

"As in Aunt Sara's Bobby?"

"Bingo!"

"Aunt Sara's current live-in boyfriend is taking my older sister to Jamaica? Where's Aunt Sara going to be for the holidays?"

"Not here. That's for sure. I don't need her moaning and wailing and accusing me of being a bad mother, your sister of being a harlot, and you of abandoning the family."

Not going there. "Did you get the package I sent?"

"Yes, but I didn't need a blouse like that."

Cora wasn't surprised the Christmas present hadn't been saved for the actual day. Impatience led her mother around by the nose. She also wasn't surprised her mother didn't like her gift.

Mom's voice whined through the car. "Did you get it on sale? Do you have the receipt? Pink is not my color. I've gone from ash blond to raven red."

"Ravens are black."

"Not the bird raven. The raving as in wild."

"Oh."

"Do you have the receipt?"

"You have the receipt. I tucked it in the box, under the tissue. You can take the blouse back to the store there in town."

"I hope I can find it."

Cora bit back a nasty retort. Her mother knew where the store was. Shopping and credit cards had a stranglehold on most of the females in her family. "I always put the receipt in, Mom."

"Don't you tell me I should have known that. Don't you say I should have looked for it. You have no call to be nitpicking at me."

"I wasn't going to say that."

"Oh yes, I know. You're too kind and generous and forgiving to actually say something negative to your mother. But you don't fool me, sister. You got too holy to say those things, but you still think them. And don't think I don't know enough about the Bible and God to know you're still guilty. If you even think something bad, you're crispy critters. Guilty as charged—thinking nasty things about your mother and your sister and the rest of your family. You might as well give it up, Cora Belle Crowder. You're no better than the rest of us once the paint peels off the banister."

"I'm getting on the freeway now, Mom. Too dangerous to talk and drive at the same time. Merry Christmas."

Cora reached down and pushed the End button. In five seconds her mother's bell tone rang again.

"Sorry, Mom," Cora said under her breath. "Traffic is treacherous on the interstate loop tonight. I need to concentrate on not smacking into disaster."

She snapped the phone shut and tossed it over her shoulder to the backseat.

8

Simon cruised through the holiday traffic with a grim attitude. How could he be such a klutz? He had the perfect opportunity to invite Cora to the ball without Sandy as an excuse. And he blew it. She'd looked at him with those big brown eyes, and he'd developed a lump in his throat the size of his fist.

One of these days, he was going to leave the horror of high school and college dating behind him. Perhaps it would be more truthful to say "attempts" at dating. With his family's enthusiastic support all his life, he hadn't realized what a stretched-out, unattractive nerd he was until he'd asked Susan Pilcher out. She didn't mind telling him that he looked like a lizard, sounded like a squeaky wheelbarrow, acted like a robot, and moved like an unfocused rubber band. He'd wondered for years what a focused rubber band moved like, then decided Susan Pilcher hadn't had as much of a flair for insults as he'd always assumed. Now he could laugh at the absurdity of it all, but it had made him wary.

His long, gangly frame hadn't filled out until two years after college. By then he was the head of his household and happy with his work. Every once in a while, a woman would catch his eye, but who would want to marry him *and* his odd family? And even more important, was there a woman out there who took a commitment to Christ as seriously as he did?

Perhaps Cora Crowder could accept his situation. He'd seen a Bible in her apartment. She had a few books by the authors he read on her bookshelves. As he turned onto his street and drove down the steep hill, he wondered what her family was like. If she'd been nurtured in the importance of family, they might share some common ground. Wait. What had she said about a soap opera? Her family lived *Tomorrow's Sorrows*. That didn't sound promising.

He came to the bridge at the bottom of the lane. The winter warning sign had been posted. "Ice on bridge. Proceed with caution." The sand truck had been by, but Simon slowed down and crossed the bridge safely. He eased up the hill and into his driveway, into his garage, out of harm's way, secure on his own territory.

He turned off the engine, then walked outside, closed the garage door, and stood breathing the cold air. He looked up at the glow of his house, each rectangle of light a beacon. He marched across the crusty snow to the back porch, opened the door, and listened to familiar sounds. Granddad humming, Aunt Mae's beads rattling, and Mom washing dishes. He didn't hear Sandy. She'd be in bed. He sighed and stepped over the threshold.

What would happen if someone from the outside came into the family? Did they really need one more person in the mix? Would someone from the outside alter the precious bond the family had? Was the risk worth it? He thought of Cora's personality. Stiff, rigid, standoffish...gentle, vulnerable...nice. Would she fit in this house? Would she want to?

Simon and Spence hoisted the Christmas tree out of the bed of the pickup truck and shouldered the prickly pine.

"Let me get this straight," said Pastor Spencer. "You're taking Sandy and a woman from work to the Wizards' Christmas Ball, but you forgot to ask the woman."

Simon started toward the nursing home with the base of the tree on his shoulder. Spence trailed behind, buried in the smaller branches. "Not exactly. Sandy asked her. Then I asked her."

"So she was asked twice, and the three of you are going together."

"I think so. Well, actually, I know we are, but I don't know if she thinks of it as a date or what, since Sandy initiated the whole thing."

"I'm not very good at the romance advice, Simon. Why don't you talk to my wife?"

"Because I already know what I should do."

"What should you do?"

Two church members held the glass doors open so Simon and the pastor could maneuver the tree into the lobby. Anchor Hill Retirement Center had remodeled the lobby since the year before, so the two puzzled over the best place to put the big tree. Once they determined the best spot, setting it up in its stand and spreading out the sheet underneath it occupied several minutes. Next, they anchored the tree to the ceiling with fishing line in case some daredevil senior citizen careened his wheelchair around a corner and into the base.

On the other side of a glass wall, in a large community room, the residents listened to Christmas carols, ate cookies, and worked on the last batch of tree ornaments. Church members mingled with the residents and helped when needed.

With the tree secured, Simon and Spence began the joyful task of untangling the strings of lights. Sandy brought them two glasses of punch and a paper plate of cookies.

"Having fun, kiddo?" asked Pastor Spencer.

"Yes sir. But I can't stay to talk. I'm in charge of Mr. Kinnaught."

"Isn't he the oldest resident?"

"Yes sir, and he keeps snitching cookies. He's only allowed three because of his diabetes. I'm supposed to keep him eating from the veggie tray instead of the sweets table."

Simon gave her a hug and kissed the top of her head. "Thanks for the cookies, Candy-Sandy. You'd better go back to your charge. I see him wheeling toward the forbidden fruit."

Sandy whirled and scurried back into the fellowship hall.

Simon and Spence took handfuls of tangled light strings and sat on the edge of the brick planter. While their fingers worked the knots out of the wires, Spence returned to his earlier question.

"What are you going to do about the ball and your uninvited guest?"

"Make sure she knows she's invited by me, that I want her to come."

"And you're going to do that by…?"

"Formally asking her to go to the ball with us." Simon held an untangled section in front of him. He saw the loop he needed to unwind next and tackled it.

Spence plugged a string of lights into the socket. It lit, so he unplugged it and began the battle against twists and snags in the line. "And you're putting this off because…?"

"She's gorgeous, and I'm a geek."

"I thought, in the story of beauty and the beast, the beast came off pretty well."

"Fairy tale." Simon laid his untangled string on a chair and selected his next challenge.

"Seems to me a date to go to a wizards' ball qualifies for some fairy-tale advantages."

"You mean like pixie dust?"

Spence shook his head. "I think pixie dust makes you fly. Not recommended on a first date."

"Remember, not everyone is clear about this being a date."

"Yes, but you are going to take care of this minor problem."

Simon let his handful of tangled lights rest in his lap as he stared at the bare evergreen tree and considered his pastor's statement. He was going to have to make a decision. Did he want to go forward developing a relationship with Cora Crowder?

Before he actually made his mouth say the words, Spence interrupted him. "The Midtown Bible Church bus has arrived. Now we can have our choir presentation."

Through the door, Simon watched the people pour out of the bus from the other church.

"Spence." He hissed under his breath.

"What?"

"That's her."

"Cora?"

"Yeah."

"Which one?"

"Black coat, red hat, and mittens."

"Whoa, boy. No wonder you're hooked."

"I'm not." Simon stood as she turned toward the building and looked through the glass wall. Their eyes met. "But I wanna be."

Cora smiled. The man who'd done such a great job of avoiding her all week at work stood in the lobby of the nursing home, with a tangle of lights in his hand and looking very much like the proverbial deer in the headlights. She hoisted the paper bag full of wrapped presents and started for the entry. Mr. Silent Gallant dropped his bundle and rushed to open the door.

She looked up at him as she passed. "Hi, Mr. Derrick. Do you have a relative here, or are you with the other church?"

"The other church. Although Granddad has friends here. My whole family is in the fellowship hall."

She had to keep moving, since more of the crew of workers were coming through behind her. "See you later."

He nodded. Still the strong, silent type.

Cora made a beeline to the gifts table and began unloading her sack. The man who'd been working with Simon came to introduce himself.

"I'm Pastor Spencer of the Northway Bible Church. I'm called Spence, and I've been a friend of Simon's for about ten years."

Cora stuck out her hand. "Pleased to meet you."

"I understand you're going to the Wizards' Christmas Ball."

Cora withdrew her hand and rearranged a pile of presents on the table. "Maybe."

"You know, it's been years since I've heard that ball mentioned. Apparently they have it every year, but it must be the best-kept secret in town."

"Do you suppose people get upset when the words 'Christmas' and 'wizards' are linked together?"

Spence put his hands in his pockets. "Could be. But the funny thing is that the only time I heard the ball mentioned was by a missionary couple who met right before the ball and ended up going to it together. Ever since Simon said he had a ticket, I've been trying to squeeze the rest of that memory out of the recesses of my mind."

"Any success? I'd like to know more about the ball's history."

"Not much, but I seem to recall the Dooghans felt God used the ball to cement their relationship and put together a man and woman to make a married team sold on doing God's business."

Cora shook her head. "That's crazy, isn't it? Usually we associate wizards with God's mandate not to have anything to do with witches and necromancers."

"Of course I'm not in favor of witches and goblins and dealing with the dead. Actually, the Anglo-Saxon term 'wizard' simply refers to older, wise people, as in 'wizened.'"

"So wizards are not closely associated with witches."

"Nope. Not inherently. But just like any other area of life, you have good and evil. One of my favorite sermons is about the evil plumber."

"What?"

"I make the point that a person's occupation doesn't determine their spiritual state. It is the condition of the heart that makes the difference. The plumber could be a nice guy or real scum. Now, of course, there are some occupations that shout the state of a person's heart."

"Like witches?" Cora asked.

"And assassins."

"And terrorists."

"Exactly. So wizards connected with the celebration of Christmas isn't necessarily impossible." He raised his eyebrows. "Well, I'll be interested to see what you and Simon have to report after the ball is over." The pastor sang the last few words.

"Spence," said Simon, appearing at Cora's elbow. "There's no call to torture members of the other church. We're supposed to be helping each other, not demoralizing the workers."

Cora put a hand on the pastor's arm. "Your singing is not that bad."

"You're too kind. It's bad enough to get me banned from the choir loft and told to mouth the words unless I turn off my lapel mike."

His face was so dour, Cora giggled.

"Your ploy for sympathy has failed, Spence." Simon put his arm around Cora's shoulders and pulled her away from his friend. "Get back to work."

The pastor turned back to the tree.

Too aware of the warmth in her cheeks, Cora moved away from Simon. "Who condemned you two to the light brigade?"

"I'm not sure. It happens every year. Somehow we also got roped into going to the lot, selecting and delivering the tree, then setting it up so that it's unlikely to fall over and bean some elderly passerby." He looked in her eyes. "Would you like to help?"

"Bean an elderly passerby? I'm not sure I'm into that sport."

He grinned and nodded toward Spence and the mountain of wires. "Untangle lights."

"Sure."

"Let me take your coat."

Cora pulled her knitted beanie off her head, wondering what havoc it had done to her hair. As she turned to allow Simon to help her off with her coat, she stuffed the hat in her pocket, along with the gloves.

She joined the team of Spencer and Derrick's Decorating Dynamos, helping to string lights and garland and climbing the ladder to hang ornaments on the higher branches. They sang Christmas carols, the youth performed a play, and then the smallest children passed out gifts to the residents of the hall. Some of the older folks retired soon after. But as the church teams cleaned up, several of the Anchor Hill staff and residents helped gather trash and tidy up.

Sandy came, wheeling her charge, Mr. Kinnaught, toward Simon and Cora as they wiped down tabletops.

"Hi, Cora! Hi, Simon!" She bubbled with enthusiasm. "Mr. Kinnaught, look who's here. Isn't she pretty? She's my friend."

Mr. Kinnaught looked over his shoulder. "I take it you're talking about the young lady and not your brother."

Sandy laughed, parked her patient at a table, and promptly pulled a water bottle out of the bag on the back of the wheelchair. She put it in front of Mr. Kinnaught.

He shook his head and took a swallow. "She's going to be the death of my kidneys. Insists I drink and drink and drink. I'm going to float into the weekend."

Sandy giggled. "He's supposed to drink a lot. But then he drinks too much. I'm supposed to keep count."

Mr. Kinnaught rubbed the back of his sleeve across his mouth. "Girl tells me she's getting a kitten for Christmas but only after Christmas, when the cat's old enough."

Sandy nodded. "We've been talking about names. I've had to say no to all Mr. Kinnaught's ideas."

Cora raised her eyebrows and looked at Simon. Simon leveled a look at the old man. "I hope your suggestions were befitting the ears of a young lady."

"You'd accuse me of saying inappropriate things to your sister?"

"I'd accuse you of being less than discreet when you get on a roll."

Mr. Kinnaught gazed at Cora. "He's my friend's grandson and thinks he can rein in my wit."

"Don't worry," said Sandy. "The worst one he came up with was Poop de Popper."

The old man growled. "It was Popper de Poop, Sandy. Get it right. Nothing wrong with calling a cat Popper."

Cora laughed at Simon's fake scowl.

Mr. Kinnaught tapped his fist on the table. "Girl also says you're going to that wizard ball. I went to it once, a long, long time ago."

"We don't know much about the ball." Cora pulled out a seat across from the old man and sat down. "Tell us about it."

Sandy sat down too and put her elbows on the table and her chin in her hands, ready to hear the story.

Mr. Kinnaught's expression softened, and his eyes seemed to see something far, far away.

"I met my Lizzy on the trolley. She had an armful of packages and the sweetest face of any angel you ever did see. I helped her carry her packages up five flights of stairs to a wee apartment, and she wouldn't let me come in." He grinned. "I stood in the door and handed her the bundles one by one. She'd go put each one down and come back for the next. I watched her walk. She had a sweet gait." He winked at Simon. "A wiggle where it ought to be."

Simon cleared his throat.

Mr. Kinnaught clucked his tongue. "Next day I won two tickets to this ball. They came in an envelope in the mail, and I couldn't even remember entering a contest. I figured my sister must have done it. It would be like her to stand next to one of those glass bowls and put the names of everyone she could think of on slips of paper and stick them in. She didn't remember any ball contest, though."

"So you took Lizzy?" asked Sandy.

"Yep, I took Lizzy. First, I courted her a bit. An ice cream soda, a walk in the snow, a picture show, and I brought her family a bakery cake on a Sunday afternoon."

Sandy squirmed in her seat. "Her family lived in the tiny apartment?"

"Nah. Her old man was a country preacher. We went out to the church, and I stayed for dinner the first week. The second week, I went out later in the day and drove Lizzy back to town."

Sandy laced her fingers together. "What about the ball, Mr. Kinnaught?"

"We got gussied up in clothes we rented from a costume shop, and we danced nearly every dance. Yes sir, that was a mighty fine shindig. And Lizzy and me, we got married in the spring."

He smiled. The memories seemed to make him happy, so Cora wanted to keep him talking.

"What did you do, Mr. Kinnaught?" asked Cora. "Your lifetime work?"

"Worked at a school. A Christian school. For fifty-two years."

Simon added, "The Brigadier Christian School of Cincinnati."

"Oh my," said Cora, "that's a very prestigious school. So many Bible scholars started there."

"Don't I know it." Mr. Kinnaught cackled. "My Lizzy mothered almost three thousand scamps and three of our own."

Cora leaned forward. "What did you do, Mr. Kinnaught?"

He winked. "I kept the halls and the dormitories clean. No Popper de Poops allowed."

While the old man laughed, Simon whispered in her ear. "He was the chaplain and then the principal."

Without warning, half the lights went out.

"Curfew," wheezed Mr. Kinnaught. "Sandy girl, walk me to my room."

"Yes sir." She stood, picked up the water bottle, then came around to the back of his chair. "Is the brake off?"

"How should I know? I'm not the driver."

Sandy checked the brake and headed out the door.

"Good night now," Mr. Kinnaught called.

"Good night," Cora and Simon echoed.

Simon made some halfhearted swipes at the already clean table with his rag. "Sounds like the ball has quite a reputation."

Cora stood and pushed in her chair. "It does."

"I have your ticket, Cora, but I'm not sure you're going. I don't want you to feel like we're forcing you to go. Sandy really wants you to go. But that's not…well…"

She looked away. What was she supposed to say?

Simon came around the table and stood right where she was looking. He took her hands and gently pulled her around to face him. She couldn't avoid his gaze without rudely turning away again.

"Cora."

Oh my, his eyes sparkled. She liked his eyes.

"I would very much like it if you accepted my invitation to come to the ball with me."

This time she knew what she was supposed to say. She grinned. "I'd love to."

9

Sandy sat on Cora's living room floor and watched the kittens in a box. They did a sort of elbow crawl around their nest, mewling for milk. Their movements reminded Cora of movies where the marines bellied under the sniper fire to gain their objective. The kittens were just as determined to get to their mother.

Skippy now tolerated people admiring her litter, and the mother cat seemed especially fond of Sandy. Cora sat on the sofa, her legs curled up, her cold feet tucked under a throw pillow. Outside, on this beautiful Saturday morning, sun sparkled off pristine snowbanks and made the tree branches glitter. Simon had deposited

Sandy with Cora for an hour and promised to bring pizza for lunch when he returned.

"But you don't have a dress," Sandy complained, with her eyes on the babies trying to stand on wobbly legs. "We should get Simon to take us to Sage Street."

"I can go to the costume shop by myself."

"He won't mind. When he picks me up, we can ask."

"We don't want to force your brother to do things. He may have other plans for this afternoon."

Sandy looked up at Cora, her beautiful eyes magnified just a bit by her thick glasses. "I wanted to come see the kittens, and Simon said he had errands. But he changed things so we could come over here. I think he likes you." She tilted her head to one side. "Do you like Simon?"

"Yes," Cora said, decisively. "I like Simon. And I like you."

"Aunt Mae says it would be good for Simon to have a woman."

Sandy cooed at the kittens, unaware that she'd set off clamoring alarms in Cora's calm morning. Cora tried to formulate a question to get a bit more information about the conversation Sandy must be remembering.

The doorbell rang. Even if she could think of a way to cross-examine Sandy without sounding like she was digging for information, her time with Simon's little sister had ended. Life was complicated.

Cora stretched the tension out of her shoulders as she stood and crossed the living room to open the door.

Simon stood on her doorstep, holding a box of pizza. Balanced on the top, a cardboard carrier held three drinks.

Cora stepped back to let him enter. "You got pizza at Meetza Pizza of Yo' Life and drinks from Creamery Delights? Why go to two places?"

Simon put the pizza on her dining room table and lifted a paper cup out of the carrier. "Because Meetza Pizza didn't have ice cream sodas. And according to Mr. Kinnaught, an ice cream soda is a necessary component of courting."

He held the cold drink out to her, and she took it automatically. Her face warmed, and her stomach fluttered.

Sandy jumped up. "I'll get plates." She went into Cora's tiny kitchen and washed her hands.

Cora looked past Simon, and his smile turned to a frown. "You look upset. Don't you like floats?"

"I think the word 'courting' has me a bit off kilter." She watched Sandy get three plates from the cupboard, then pull out a stack of napkins and three forks.

Watching Sandy efficiently handle the chore gave Cora something to admire. Something to distract her. Distraction was good, right? Especially when she felt flustered and out of her depth. The way this conversation had started diametrically opposed how she thought their relationship would begin. Slow. Cautious. Beating around the bush for months.

Not like this. Not like one day he's my boss's boss and the next, he's my beau.

She preferred beating around the bush for months.

"I've asked you out on a date. Do you prefer the word 'dating' over 'courting'?"

Cora swallowed. Simon's voice had gone stiff. She'd heard him talk to employees when he was displeased, and he never sounded anything but cordial. But he'd just gone cold with her. She risked a quick glance and saw the muscles in his jaw working.

Sandy brought in the plates and set the table quickly. "Give me your coat, Simon, and I'll hang it up."

Her brother complied, silently. Sandy walked off with his blue parka.

Cora felt the need to say something. She prepared herself for the onslaught that would surely come. Stiff muscles strangled her throat. She managed to speak, but her eyes would not look above the buttons on his shirt. "I've never dated much. I'm not good at it."

She heard a whoosh of air as Simon seemed to deflate. "I haven't either. But I don't believe in casual dating. You know, the kind portrayed in movies and on TV."

Sandy pulled out a chair next to Cora and gently pushed her into it. "We don't watch TV, Simon."

"Well, that's one of the reasons we don't." He sat in the chair Sandy pointed to.

Sandy circled the table and sat on the other side. She took Simon's hand and then Cora's and bowed her head. Without allowing her eyes to meet his, Cora stretched her arm toward Simon. Tension ebbed out of her body when his large hand gently cradled hers.

Sandy prayed, "Dear Jesus, thank You for this pizza and the ice cream sodas. Help Simon and Cora look at You and only You. Forgive me for wanting the kitten now. I know it would be bad to take one away from its mama this soon. Help me wait. Help me decide on which kitten. Help me find a good name. Amen."

Sandy looked up and smiled. "I love pizza."

"I do too." Cora opened the box. "Oh my! This is my favorite kind!"

Sandy laughed out loud. "That's why I got the forks. Simon always gets Mount Much-More."

Cora gestured for Sandy to hand over her plate. "I'll have to slide the plate under to catch the shifting veggies and meat."

She served Simon next and then got a slice for herself. She took a sip of the ice cream soda. "Mmm! What kind is this?"

Simon talked out of the side of his mouth, successfully hiding the pizza he chewed. "Two scoops of chocolate in black-cherry cream soda."

"It's delicious." Cora took another large draw on her straw. "Yikes!" Pain radiated through her sinuses. "Yeow!"

"Brain freeze," declared Sandy. "Save her, Simon. Save her!"

Simon jumped from his seat, stood behind Cora, and placed his hands over her face. "Don't worry. I'm a professional." His index fingers pushed down under her eyes. His thumbs pressed against her temples. He gently massaged in an up-and-down motion.

"Better?" he whispered in her ear.

A pleasant haze replaced the pain. "Yes."

"You have to take tiny sips," Sandy said.

Cora nodded ever so carefully. She didn't want to interrupt the soothing massage.

"When you forget," continued Sandy in a rather irritating, officious tone, "you get a brain freeze."

Simon's fingers stopped, and his hands dropped down to Cora's shoulders where small circular motions with his thumbs did another kind of magic. "Don't be such a know-it-all, Sandy. Remember? The tone of voice we use can be offensive."

"Kettle black," said Sandy.

Cora opened her eyes to see sweet Sandy glaring at her brother. The pot calling the kettle black. What was she referring to?

Simon patted Cora's shoulder and sat down. "Sandy's right. I owe you an apology, Cora. I spoke to you in anger."

Cora's eyes popped open. Their little discussion about courting? That was anger?

She grinned at the absurdity. Her family could show them what a real fight sounded like. The next thought erased her smile. "Am I supposed to apologize to you too? Did I sound like a fishwife?"

Sandy burst into laughter. "What's a fishwife? A lady married to a fish?"

"More like a woman married to someone who fishes commercially," Cora explained. "She takes his catch and goes up and down the streets, yelling for people to come out and buy the fish."

"People really do that?"

"I really don't think they do it anywhere anymore. I know they did it in England years ago. The women had shrill voices and used crude language. That's why if you sound like an argumentative woman, someone might call you a fishwife."

"I don't think Simon would call you a fishwife. But he doesn't like arguing. No one in our family does. 'A gentle answer turns away wrath, but a harsh word stirs up anger.'" Sandy took a sip of her ice cream soda. "I'm not good at my tone all the time. Simon has to remind me." Then she grinned. "So I get to remind him sometimes too."

Cora shook her head slowly. "That's amazing."

Sandy took a big bite of pizza, and a word came out that sounded something like "Whuh?"

"Why? Because my family never stops arguing. None of them are Christian. I'm sort of the white sheep. Growing up, I spent a lot of time in my closet with my head under blankets to muffle the noise of the fights.

"I loved school because if you fought, you had to go to the principal's office, so the classrooms were more or less peaceful. I did really well at school, so I got scholarships to go to college." Cora paused. "That was when my mother kicked me out."

Simon frowned at her. "Why'd she do that?"

"I'd gotten too uppity. No one was teaching me about the soft-answer thing. I wasn't as feisty as my siblings, or as loud, but I certainly knew a better vocabulary. And my mom thought I used the grand words to prove I was better than them. She didn't like that."

Sandy's big eyes pooled tears of compassion. "She threw you out. Did that make you sad?"

"Actually, it was kind of a relief. I didn't have to report in and maybe get backhanded."

Sandy's eyes flew to Simon's face.

He nodded. "Yes, that means they hit her."

Sandy gasped. "That's horrible."

Cora smiled at her dismay. "Well, it is, but I didn't know it was horrible, because that was just part of my normal life." She patted Sandy's arm. "Don't worry about it. The story gets better."

"Oh good." Sandy took another big bite.

Simon looked at Cora. "Will you tell us, please?"

"I went to the college, but my scholarship didn't cover housing. I told the academic advisor that I would probably have to drop my classes. She said to wait, and she gave me five dollars to go get a sandwich. When I came back in a few hours, she had found a home that would take me in. And that's when God put His hand on me and said, 'Here I am.'"

"Wow!" Sandy wiped her hands on her napkin and reached for a second piece of Mount Much-More pizza. "I've always had a Christian family. I'm glad."

The laden pizza wedge wobbled in her hand, threatening to dump the mountain of veggies and meat. Simon grabbed Sandy's plate and rescued her from the avalanche. She grinned and picked up her fork to tackle the mangled mess in front of her.

Cora steered the conversation away from herself and asked Sandy questions about her life.

"I like working with old people," Sandy said. "Little kids are too quick and get away from you. I help in the church preschool sometimes, and those kids are just everywhere at once. So mostly I work in the Mountain Climbers' room."

"Mountain Climbers?"

Simon laughed. "Senior citizens. They named their own group. They say that ever since they made it over the hill, all the other hills seem like mountains. So they are the Mountain Climbers."

Cora chuckled. "At least they still have their sense of humor. But Sandy, what do you do in there?"

"Lots of things. I pick up things they drop on the floor. I help them find stuff. Now that it's winter, they wear tons of clothes, and

I help them put on all those sweaters and jackets and heavy coats and gloves and scarves and hats and boots. I help them get buttoned and zipped and to the right door to meet their families. They really need me." Sandy cast Cora a sly grin. "And they're too slow to get away."

"And," said Simon, "they love her to pieces."

Sandy beamed and nodded her head.

When they could not eat one more bite, Simon stored the rest of the pizza in the fridge.

"Let's go." Sandy had already picked up her coat.

Simon peeked out of the kitchen. "Go where?"

"To get Cora's dress."

Cora didn't think about the tone of her voice. It lowered on its own accord and came out in a slow rumble. "Sannnndeee."

"It's all right, Cora." Simon walked out of the kitchen. "Do you have something else planned?"

She took a deep breath. Simon was going to be reasonable. She could be reasonable too. It might take a lot of practice to learn to be as reasonable as he was, but she was going to try. "No, but maybe you do. I told Sandy not to force you into going."

"I did my Christmas shopping this morning. As long as Sandy doesn't look in the trunk..."

Sandy's eyes brightened.

Simon grinned. "We can go shopping."

"Hurray!" his sister shouted.

"And come to think of it, I need to get a costume as well."

Cora cocked an eyebrow at him.

"I thought I could fit into a costume I had from a play eight years ago, but…um…my physique has changed a bit." Simon pointed a finger at Sandy. "Let's *ask* Cora if she would like to spend her afternoon with us."

"Would you?" Sandy's face read like a book. Cora could see that the girl was praying silently for a positive answer.

Cora put Sandy out of her misery. "Yes, I'll come. Walking along Sage Street is just the thing to work off some of that delicious lunch."

"Get your coat," ordered Sandy. "And everyone better take a bathroom break before we go." She threw her coat back on the couch before heading down the hall.

Cora caught Simon looking at her out of the corner of his eye, waiting for her reaction.

She shrugged. "Well, she's right."

They both burst out laughing. Simon took a moment to stop chuckling. He crouched beside the kittens and stroked each in turn with one large finger. "Has she shown any preferences?"

"She prefers them all."

"An equal-opportunity kitty lover."

"Sandy's very sweet."

Simon nodded. "Most of the time."

Most of the time? Hey, that meant even Sandy didn't achieve the higher walk all the time.

Simon and his sister drove her nuts. Of course, they knew more about the right way to celebrate Christmas, and she took the opportunities to observe and catch their method. But their example of being nonjudgmental emphasized her shortcomings. Maybe training herself to be a good Christian was a hopeless task.

She casually glanced at the two as they prepared to go out in the cold.

They made Christianity look so easy. Could it really be easy?

Simon excused himself and headed down the hall. Sandy slipped into her coat and struggled to get the zipper started.

"Need help?" asked Cora.

"No, thanks. It's just old and getting stubborn."

The zipper cooperated, and Sandy grinned. "Simon says you'd make a great mother."

Cora thought her eyebrows would shoot off the top of her head. "He does?"

Sandy put her hand over her mouth and giggled. "He does!"

10

"It's got to be here someplace." Sandy's plaintive whine pinched Simon's already irritated nerves. Traffic downtown reminded him of the tangled light strings he and Spence had unraveled at the nursing home.

Cora looked over her shoulder from the passenger seat. "You're right. It has to be here. A whole street doesn't just disappear. Navigating this traffic is like trying to brush a tiger's teeth."

Simon spied Sandy's puzzled expression in the rearview mirror.

Cora laughed. "Maybe that's not the best simile. I had a picture in my mind of the cars being the tiger's teeth. We're trying to maneuver through them without getting snapped."

"Floss," said Simon from behind the wheel. "Slipping in and out between the cars."

Cora wrinkled her nose. "That's not a very appealing simile either."

"What's a simile?" asked Sandy. She looked to Cora for an answer.

"When you compare something to something else to get a better picture of it in your head. The clouds look like cotton balls. The edge of the snow shovel is sharp like a knife. You usually use the word 'like' in the comparison."

Sandy squinted her eyes and pursed her lips. "She held the doll like a baby. Kids like candy."

Cora chuckled. "The first one is a simile, but the second just says what kids do. They like candy. To make it a simile the kids would have to be like candy in some way. The kids were sweet like candy."

"Okay." Sandy concentrated. After a minute she opened her eyes wide. "The ketchup looked like a line of blood on the hot dog."

Simon and Cora laughed.

"Good," said Simon, "but kind of morbid."

Sandy giggled. "Morbid is creepy, isn't it?"

"Yes."

"I'll try again." She thought for a minute. "They sat in the front seat like a husband and wife."

Simon did not comment on the sentence. Was Sandy coy or clueless? Better not delve into the possibilities.

"Similes can also use the word 'as.' The poinsettia was as red as…" Cora paused. "Oh good night, what's the same shade of red as a poinsettia?"

"Your face," Simon supplied.

He interpreted Cora's look to mean, "Watch it, buster."

Before she could respond, Sandy spoke up. "I want to do one."

Simon spotted his destination. "Too late. We're here."

Cora looked out the front window. "At work?"

"At the parking garage. We can walk faster than we can drive through that traffic. And where did we think we were going to park once we got there?"

"Brilliant," said Sandy. "No more wasted time in the car."

Simon felt the same way, except he had been enjoying the game of making similes with Sandy and the comfortable presence of his new friend.

Simon escorted Cora as they walked through the crowd of holiday shoppers. Sandy preferred to examine the store windows up close. Simon kept an eye on her so she didn't wander too far ahead or stop to gaze into a display while they walked on.

Downtown's renovated district provided lots of opportunities to spend money. Simon expected Cora to be window shopping, but she seemed content to walk on, glancing in the windows and, more often, watching people. She did stop at a display Sandy wanted her to see. Simon didn't find the miniature ceramic village interesting enough to stand and ogle it.

"Let's keep moving," he said. "The perfect dress awaits." He dislodged Cora from the window by putting her arm through his and giving a slight tug. Sandy followed.

Having Cora's gloved hand tucked in his arm felt right. Had she really worked at Sorenby's for five years? Of course, he'd known she was part of his staff for a long time. After all, he read the reviews. He had a passing thought once in a while that she was a good employee. But he'd never noticed the honey color of her hair, the dimple near the right corner of her mouth, or her brown eyes. That expression of merriment that sometimes brightened her face literally awakened something joyful in his staid and proper heart.

Snow sifted down from gray clouds like fine powdered sugar. He squeezed Cora's arm. "Ice cream soda, a walk in the snow."

She looked up at him, startled, then smiled.

He pointed to Sandy in front of a shoe shop to deflect her attention. What was the matter with him? Doing the romantic bit was totally out of his league. Words popped out of his mouth before he even knew he was thinking them and made him sound like a fool. He'd figured he had blown it again with that last inane statement. At least he hadn't mentioned courtship again.

Cora matched his pace, and they walked together with easy companionship.

They turned into Sage Street, and the crowd immediately thinned. Simon stopped and turned to look back. Throngs of people crossed the intersection without even looking their way.

The light changed colors. The people stopped. From the other direction, pedestrians crossed the street, coming toward them, then turned off in either direction. Not even one person continued into this part of Sage. Cars, rather old cars, were parallel parked on either side in front of the shops, but none of the cars on the cross street turned down this block.

"Just a minute, Cora. I want to conduct an experiment. Watch Sandy for me, will you?"

He barely caught the puzzled frown on her face, but he heard her "Of course."

Simon strode back to the crowded intersection and watched the faces of those who passed by. It wasn't his imagination. They all ignored this side street. He looked over at Cora and saw that Sandy had come to stand beside her. They both watched him. He gave a little wave he hoped was reassuring.

A man dressed in an expensive black overcoat and a stylish, stingy-brim fedora approached from the other direction.

Simon held out his hand. "Sir."

The man glanced up.

"Could you tell me if there's a bookstore down that street?" Simon waved toward Cora and his sister.

The man paused, frowned, and pointed in the opposite direction. "There's a big chain store two blocks over. Has a coffee shop, and I believe they're having a string quartet play Christmas music this afternoon."

Simon shook his head. "No, I'm looking for a small shop in that direction."

The man's frown deepened, then he shook his head and moved on.

Simon bit his lower lip. *Do these people not see the street we do? Impossible!*

Next he stopped a teenage couple. They told him of a classic comics store, but paid no attention to the street he pointed out. He stopped an old man and, with relief, heard him say he remembered a small bookstore down that way.

"Have you been there lately?" Simon asked.

The old man grinned and walked off.

He'd try one more time.

A mother and two children trudged past. The woman carried a younger, sleeping girl on her shoulder. The older girl plodded beside her mom. They put one foot in front of the other, looking weary.

"Excuse me." Simon smiled and held his hands out in a help-less gesture. "I'm looking for a quaint little bookshop. I was told there was one on Sage Street." He pointed toward the two women he was supposed to be taking to see the Booterbaw sisters. "Do you know if there's a bookstore that way?"

The woman sighed, and her eyes followed Simon's gesture. Her face lost some of its fatigue. "Oh my, how lovely." She tugged gently on the older girl's arm. "Let's go down this street. It's charming." She hitched the sleeping child higher on her shoulder. "And not crowded. Maybe we can find a place to rest and have a snack." She walked on to Sage Street, apparently forgetting Simon and his question.

Simon watched the small family walk past Sandy and Cora, then focused his gaze beyond and studied the street.

The shops and cars, and even most of the people, looked like they belonged together in some movie set meant to look like the forties or fifties. Except the cars weren't so old, and the pedestrians weren't wearing odd clothing.

Simon responded to Sandy's beckoning wave, but his mind kept working on the conundrum. Every time he thought he'd put his finger on what made the street so peculiar, he found he'd missed details that didn't quite fit his assessment.

Cora's eyes sparkled as he came closer. "What were you doing?"

"Let's go," said Sandy at the same time.

Simon took Cora's hand, and they strolled after his sister.

"I was trying to see if everyone can see this street."

"What?" Cora's face mirrored the bewilderment he felt.

Had he actually thought some people didn't see this part of Sage? What was the shopping district? Make-believe? No, he might call it unusual reality, but he'd not go so far as to proclaim fantasy here. The pavement felt solid beneath his feet. He heard city traffic and the chattering of people walking by. He smelled…a bakery. He stopped.

The woman and her two girls sat on the other side of a large glass window. The mother looked at a menu. Simon read the lettering on the window. "Faerie Cake Bakery."

He squeezed Cora's hand. "What are faerie cakes?"

"A light cake. Usually it's a cupcake, with adornments on the top. Sometimes the cake itself has a citrus zest added."

"Adornments?"

"Nuts or fruit for adults, a dab of icing and sprinkles for kids." Cora raised their linked hands and pointed at the window display. "Sometimes a face made of candies."

Simon peered down at Cora. "How do you know these things?"

"The family I lived with during college cooked. Well, I guess most families cook, but they hardly ever went out to eat, and everyone would pile into the kitchen and have fun making stuff. Everything from spaghetti meat loaf to soda bread from an old Irish recipe."

"Spaghetti meat loaf?"

"I know it sounds awful, but it was quite good. The smallest son suggested they put the meatball on the outside and the spaghetti inside." Cora cocked her head. "So did you find out if only some people can see Sage Street?"

"Inconclusive. No one said, 'Are you crazy? There's no street in that direction.' But some of them looked at me as if I were crazy."

"That could just be a city dweller's natural reaction to being spoken to when he or she is minding his or her own business. And a hint to you to mind *your* own business."

Simon didn't take offense. She offered her opinion with a sweet smile, and he was encouraged that she had relaxed out of the employee-to-boss mode. He squeezed her hand once more.

They started walking again. Sandy had paused several stores farther down the street.

Simon twisted his lips. "A toy store? I don't remember a toy store."

"Maybe you weren't looking for a toy store."

"I don't remember seeing the Faerie Cake Bakery either."

"I *know* you weren't looking for faerie cakes."

Simon laughed. "No, I wasn't."

She giggled, and the soft sound eased the tightness in his neck and relaxed the worry muscles around his eyes. Simon realized he held her hand and, at the same time, realized that it felt natural and that he had been holding it for some time. Even gripping it gently when something felt good.

The act of engaging a woman's affection had never been comfortable before. When had he taken hold of her hand? He couldn't even remember.

They stopped walking when they came up behind Sandy.

"Aren't they wonderful?" Sandy sighed. "All these old dolls. I bet they're the kind of dolls people collect and put on shelves instead of playing with 'em."

"Would you like to collect dolls, Sandy?" Cora asked the question Simon had just formulated in his head.

"No." She turned her angelic smile on Simon and Cora. "I want a kitten to cuddle, not a doll I can't touch."

Simon placed an arm around Sandy's back. "Very wise, my pixie girl."

Sandy accepted the compliment with a nod of her head.

The snow left off being gentle and dainty. Large flakes descended in increasing numbers.

"I think it's time," said Simon, "for us to hone in on the costume shop and quit getting sidetracked."

The number of pedestrians thinned even more as the snowfall intensified, and the three dashed for the comfort of the store.

11

Bonnie and Betty Booterbaw welcomed Sandy and Cora like long-lost friends. Simon was relieved to get a less effusive greeting from the two lady costumers.

Bonnie pulled Cora toward a rack of clothes. "I'm guessing these dresses are about your size. Let's get to work. We're closing the shop early tonight, because Betty and I have dinner engagements with our beaus." She glanced at her sister and blushed.

"Don't look at me, Bonnie. You didn't have to tell." Betty took Simon's arm and steered him toward the door. "It's going to take us at least an hour to pick the right dress for your friend. And it will only take ten minutes for you to choose an outfit. Why don't you go visit some of the other stores?"

Bonnie giggled. "She means you'll be in the way, and your pretty friend may want to surprise you with the gown she wears."

A cat jumped down from a cabinet and twined around his legs. The air in the room seemed too hot and dry after the cold, snowy wind outside. Simon watched his sister and his "pretty friend" examine the dresses, exclaiming over colors and fabrics. Cora probably would take longer to decide on a costume than his easily pleased sister. A whole hour in this place would be tedious. Roaming the curious street was a much better alternative.

"Right," said Simon, making a beeline for the door. "I'll be back in an hour."

He pulled out his cell phone as he walked. He tapped speed dial and soon heard a ring.

"Hello. Greg Spencer at Ohgoodgrief Fellowship of Wobbly Christians."

"Very funny, Spence. You've been awful since you got caller ID. The elders should vote to take it away from you."

"Man, your signal is crackly, Simon. Where are you?"

"Sage Street."

"Oh, the part that doesn't exist? That would explain the weak signal."

"It exists, Spence. I'm walking down Sage right now." Simon

stopped and turned a full circle. This outdoor mall, or whatever it was, was real.

"Why are you on Sage Street?"

"I brought Sandy and Cora shopping."

"So you officially asked the young lady out."

"Yes, and I bought her an ice cream soda, and we've been for a walk in the snow."

Silence answered him from Spence's end.

"Spence?"

"I'm trying to catch up. Ice cream soda and a walk in the snow?"

"Yes, and I'm going to ask her to go to a picture show tomorrow evening when Sandy is busy with her church group."

"Ice cream soda. A walk in the snow. Picture show. Is this some old song I can't remember?"

"No, it's 'sort-of' advice from Mr. Kinnaught at the nursing home."

"Okay, buddy, I'd like to humor you, but I have a visitation to make. Why'd you call?"

Simon stood still under the awning of a flower shop. Why *had* he called his best friend? To tell him he was falling in love? To tell him he was *afraid* he was falling in love? To say he'd gotten claustrophobic in a shop that hadn't bothered him before? To say he'd gotten claustrophobic because he was too comfortable with and getting too close to a young woman he barely knew? Maybe to admit he was rushing toward a permanent commitment and needed some cautionary words.

But he didn't want cautionary words. He wanted reassurance that he, too, was allowed to fall in love and score an incredible wife. That he knew this was what he wanted. Maybe he'd come to the right circumstances and found the right woman. Perhaps he'd decided to pursue this course, and now he needed encouragement.

"I called to say Merry Christmas, Spence. Merry Christmas!"

"Well, that's a hill of beans. We'll talk tomorrow. Meanwhile, pray I have the right words to comfort a hurting mother and father. See you in church."

"Will do." Simon snapped his cell phone shut and slipped it into his pocket. He sent up a quick prayer for his friend to minister to the parents he had an appointment with, then glanced up and down the street, trying to decide where he should hang out while waiting for the girls.

He didn't know what to do with the immediate future or what to do with long-range future. These questions should be fairly easy to address. Follow God's direction, plain and simple. Now, to do it. Simon strolled east on Sage, confident that, at least, that action was not out of God's will.

"I think she should be a butterfly." Bonnie pulled out a set of wings, brightly colored with black vein markings and big spots. "We have lots of these in different colors, Cora. You choose the dress you want, and then we match the wings."

Betty pulled out a different sort of wing set. "These are fairy wings. I've always preferred fairy wings." The gossamer fabric over an almost invisible frame had no markings but the material glimmered and shifted shades as Betty moved the wings.

Sandy looked up from where she petted a gray cat. "I like them both."

"So do I." Cora looked from one Booterbaw sister to the other and then sighed. "Let's pick the dress first. I really don't think I can afford wings."

Bonnie patted her shoulder. "We'll see, dear. Some of the dresses come with a free wing rental. You keep the dress and bring back the wings. After all, most people don't have much use for wings, except to wear them to a wizards' ball."

"Do you suppose fairies came to Bethlehem to see baby Jesus?" asked Sandy.

"If fairies really exist," said Betty, "then, of course, they would come. Every creature invited by the Father would want to worship the Son of God. But that doesn't mean that anyone would have seen them other than God, His Son, and maybe the angels."

"So," said Bonnie, "we wouldn't know. A lot of things are like that. Sometimes we don't know what dealings God has with a person until right before a person dies."

Sandy turned to look at Bonnie. "My father died. We know he went to heaven." She stroked the cat's fur. "But our neighbor, Mr. Winston, died, and we don't know if he went to heaven."

"That's just what I mean," Bonnie said as she straightened a gown in danger of falling off its hanger. "We look at someone and don't know. God looks in Mr. Winston's heart, and God knows. And I think God sits some of those folks down right before they die and brings to mind all the clues that person has been given about Himself. Maybe He says, 'When you think of all those facts in one breath of fresh air, do you still want to ignore Me?'"

"Maybe," Betty agreed. "God doesn't do things our way, you know. He does them His way."

As Cora flipped through the rack of gowns, she thought about the sisters' easy discussion of God mixed with talk of fairies. They stood strong in their belief in God and Jesus. Yet they did not cast fairies into a black pit with demons and witches. How did that work? She hadn't been a Christian long enough to encounter this attitude of complete trust. *He does them His way.* And they obviously trusted Him to do things right. How far did their philosophy reach?

"You said you don't do much business at Halloween?"

"Dear," said Betty firmly, "we are not that type of costume shop. We carry the same stock all year. School plays use our goods more than trick-or-treaters. Many girls come here for their prom dresses."

Cora believed that mothers and fathers would be vastly relieved to have their teenagers pick from these gorgeous but modest gowns. On the other hand, none of the girls she'd gone to high school with would have chosen from these racks.

"But if you want to do ghouls and dead things—"

"Or near-dead things," interjected Bonnie, "you'll have to go to one of those cheap stores that have no commitment to art."

"Costuming is an art," Betty added. "And we believe that catering to the darker nature of mankind is unwise. We concentrate on beauty."

Cora had to agree. The artistry in these costumes far exceeded the most expensive of scary Halloween attire. But she still didn't know how they kept their prices so ridiculously low.

After trying on nearly a dozen dresses, they narrowed their choices down to two. Sandy ignored the proceedings as she made friends with one cat after another, but when called upon to help with the final decision, she voted for the azure blue gown Cora modeled.

"I like the sleeves," she said.

Cora held out her arms, and diaphanous streamers of fabric floated down from the seam along the back of her arm from the wrist to shoulder.

The bell on the front door jangled, and Cora dove into the dressing room.

She heard Sandy tell her brother they were almost ready, so he'd better pick his costume.

"You can forget putting me in leggings like Prince Charming, Sandy."

Sandy giggled. "You can be a court jester. I saw a funny hat and balloony, baggy, clown pants over there."

"Why can't I be a prince who wears normal pants?"

"Here," said Bonnie, "look at these. You won't be embarrassed to wear them."

Cora wanted badly to peek, but she also didn't want to be seen, and until Betty or Bonnie came to unbutton her, she couldn't get out of the dress.

She gave up trying to hear every word and turned to survey herself in the three-paneled mirror. The blue gown fit her beautifully. She felt gorgeous. Her heart zinged.

"I'm pretty enough to go with the handsome and exceedingly efficient boss man." She tilted her head and continued to admire her image as she pondered the situation.

She had the approaching opportunity to stand in for Mrs. Hudson. What if someone in the office thought she'd used Simon to get that job? Maybe she shouldn't be going with Simon and his sister to the Wizards' Christmas Ball. Maybe this was one of those small things that bloomed into disaster. In her family one little misstep could lead to explosions of emotion that had long-range repercussions.

But she'd moved into a different life with a different Person in authority—and that Person was not her mother.

The curtain moved aside behind her, and Bonnie poked her head in. "Oh dear, you look like you just saw a car crash." She tilted her head and looked seriously at her customer. "You have that alarmed look, one caused by a very unpleasant thought about something that might not even happen. Those unpleasantries don't usually happen, you know. What were you thinking about, dear Cora?"

"Catastrophe," she whispered.

"Well, stop it." Bonnie began unbuttoning the dress. "Just stop it."

12

Mr. Kinnaught had not mentioned dinner as part of his courtship of Lizzy, but after a late-afternoon matinee, Simon figured Cora would be as hungry as he was. They walked out of the theater into the mall, which was decorated with snowmen and reindeer.

"I had thought to ask you if you wanted to grab a bite to eat at the food court, but this all seems too bright and flashy."

Cora quirked an eyebrow. "After watching the Spanish hero save his true love's family, I'm craving Mexican."

"I know a good place for Mexican. Spence and I have made it one of our premier concerns to investigate the lesser-known eateries of our fair city." Simon pulled her arm through his and laced his fingers through hers as he started walking toward the exit. "How does a Mexican meal prepared by an Englishman named Leland sound?" He paused. "Leland means 'fallow ground' in Old English."

Cora laughed. "How did you know that?"

"Leland is my middle name."

"What does Simon mean?"

"Simon means 'He has heard.' I guess my parents thought that if 'Simon has heard' the Word that fell on 'fallow ground,' I'd turn out all right."

"That's a Bible verse, right?"

"There's two, but this is the one they meant: 'For thus saith the LORD to the men of Judah and Jerusalem, Break up your fallow ground, and sow not among thorns.'"

"Old Testament?"

"Yes, Jeremiah 4, verse 3."

"So what does it mean to you?"

"God has given us good resources; use them. Don't choose the thorny or sin-laden fields because those are not meant for His people."

Cora smiled at him. He liked her smile. He'd have to admit he even enjoyed the romantic movie, just because she had sat beside him.

The heavy traffic guaranteed they were hungry by the time they finally reached Leland's, quite a stark difference from when he'd been here for lunch with Spence. Simon said a thank-you to God for providing the ambiance he hadn't even considered. Leland's provided the perfect backdrop for a date with a beautiful woman. The evening atmosphere of the place catered to romantic dinners. Candles glowed in glass snifters on each table, and the lower lights and the soft music of Spanish guitars blended well with hushed conversations.

The hostess sat them in a booth and handed out menus. Cora suddenly laughed.

"What?"

"Listen."

Simon concentrated on the sounds around him. Then he smiled. "Would you call that 'O Little Town of Bethlehem, Cha-cha-cha'?"

"It's strange, but kind of catchy."

He watched her face. Her expressions hid nothing. Her eyes said she was having fun. Simon relaxed and listened as she talked.

"I suppose many songs cross borders and take on the flavor of whatever country they land in."

He agreed, but his mind was traveling in many different directions at once. Had he ever felt this comfortable with a woman in such a short amount of time? Had he ever let himself be this open?

They ordered, then talked about movies they'd seen, authors they admired, and places they wanted to go. The delicious meal got some of their attention, but the conversation was more important than the spicy food.

Cora pushed a small amount of Spanish rice left on her plate into a pile. "I want to ask you something."

"Go ahead."

"Why are you so different outside the office? You have two personalities: Mr. Serious Simon Derrick and this one. I like this one, but I never would have guessed you were so much fun."

"Focus." Simon put his napkin down on the table. "My father had this thing about focusing. He drilled it into me and my brother. When you mowed the lawn, you focused on your job. Were there twigs in the way, stray rocks from the edging, small toys in the tall grass? Any of them could fly up and hit you if you ran over them. When we went fishing, we focused on water safety. When we did homework, we were encouraged to focus on the subject at hand. No playing the radio while we studied. And he particularly insisted that you gave your all at work, because your employer was paying your wages. If he paid you for an hour of work, don't short him by a minute here and a minute there while your mind wanders to other things."

"Your father sounds like a hard taskmaster."

Simon shook his head. "Not a bit. He focused on his children, on his family, in just the same dedicated way. When I came to him with a problem, I got the undivided attention I needed. I hope to be as good a parent as he was."

"What happened?"

"A drunk driver. Both my dad and my brother died. The other driver did as well."

"How long ago?"

"Fifteen years."

"I'm sorry."

Her empathy reached like fingers into his soul and caressed that old childhood pain. A seed of contentment sprouted in Simon's heart. He took her hand. Did he dare entrust himself to this delicate creature? She watched him, waiting for him to speak.

"I guess I've been rather busy living up to his expectations, trying to be the man of his house. Sandy recently pointed out that it's time for me to be the man of my own house."

"Is that what you want?"

He shrugged. "I'm beginning to. I'm thirty."

"Old man." She put on a sympathetic face.

He grinned at her. "Then Sandy informed me that when I became the man of my own house, the family would sell the old place and move in with me and my new family so I could still boss her around."

"Is *that* what you want?"

"It wouldn't bother me, but being that close with the in-laws would probably be culture shock for most women in America."

"Not all women."

That statement caught his attention. He wanted her to love

family and enjoy nurturing as he did. In talks with Spence, he'd identified that caring for his younger sister and his older relatives helped define who he was. "I am planted in a multigenerational home."

Her eyes narrowed, and she thought for a moment before making a comment. "That would be a hard circumstance for some people to embrace. But you're right about it being a cultural thing. In many other societies, clans live together." She paused. "I wonder what God thinks of the whole idea. I don't believe there's a verse in the Bible that says, 'Thou shalt harbor your kin for better or worse.'" Her eyes dropped down to her plate, and she pulled her hand away from him.

Before Simon could investigate this sudden retreat, the waitress came to clear away the dishes and offer dessert.

"I suggest fried ice cream and Mexican coffee. Both are sweet, and Leland imports the cinnamon from Mexico."

"I'm too full," said Cora.

Simon winked at the waitress and addressed his date. "How about having coffee, and I'll get the ice cream? You can have a taste, and if it reawakens your appetite, I'll share."

He was rewarded when a smile returned to Cora's face.

"Two Mexican coffees, one fried ice cream, and two spoons."

"Wait." Cora blushed. "What is Mexican coffee?"

The server laughed. "Ours has chocolate, cinnamon, vanilla, brown sugar, and whipped cream on top."

Cora raised her eyebrows. "And coffee?"

"Yes, organic beans from Mexico."

"It sounds delicious."

"Oh, you'll like it all righty." The young waitress left to fill the order.

"You're feeding my addiction to international cuisine," Cora said as the waitress moved away.

Simon laughed out loud. "I'll take that as a challenge to take you out more often and to different ethnic restaurants. Ever try Ethiopian?"

Finally. Cora leaned back against the comfortable cushions in the passenger seat, closed her eyes, and said a prayer of thanks. Finally, she'd met a man who didn't drink, didn't cuss, didn't make suggestive remarks, didn't have his hands all over her. Finally, she'd met a man who treated his family well, went to church, talked about his faith, and was kind, considerate, and courteous.

Any minute she would wake up, right?

They pulled into her apartment complex, and Simon parked near the entrance to her building.

"I'll walk you up," he said as he opened his door. He came around to her side and tucked her arm in his. The maintenance man had swept the sidewalks earlier, but a new layer of snow dusted the pavement, and the walk sparkled in the lights from streetlamps along the way. They came to the door to her building, and Cora inserted her badge in the slot. The light flickered and the lock clicked. Simon pulled it open.

They both stomped on the snow pad at their feet, shaking off most of the packed snow sticking to their shoes.

"There are parts of winter I don't like," said Simon.

"Like what?"

"Taking my shoes off at the back door, walking through the kitchen with only socks on, and stepping on a clod of snow left by someone else who's been outside."

Cora made a face and shook her head. "Never happens at my place."

A burst of laughter and the sudden onslaught of a very loud Christmas tune filled the hallway.

Cora smiled. "It sounds like the Bakers in 1A are having a party."

"I agree. Sounds like merriment of the finest measure." He turned her toward the stair. "Okay, what do you not like about winter?"

"Easy one. Sliding into curbs and breaking tie rods. You don't have to come up."

"I'll see you to your door. Just in case someone is lurking in the halls."

Cora harrumphed. "No one is lurking in the halls."

"Okay, then I'm not ready to part with your company."

She giggled. "You are such a smooth talker."

They trudged up the steps and turned into the second-floor hallway. Cora stopped so suddenly, Simon bumped into her.

"What are you doing here?" she asked.

A young woman dressed in a long, elegant coat, stylish fur helmet, and high-heeled boots sat on an upturned suitcase. "Merry Christmas to you too."

"You're not staying here."

Simon's breath tickled the back of Cora's neck. "Someone you know?"

Cora tried to subdue the bile that rose as the woman stood. The unwanted guest's eyes narrowed, and she gazed at Simon with a come-hither look.

"I'd introduce you," Cora said, "but I don't know what she's currently using for a name."

Cora's nemesis laughed, stepped forward, and extended her hand. "I'm Zee. Cora's sister."

Simon reached around to take Zee's hand, but as he did so, he put a possessive arm around Cora's shoulders. "I don't believe she was expecting a visit."

Zee grasped his hand and looked past Cora, deliberately employing her best man-snatching expression. Simon withdrew his hand, and some look on his face must have disengaged her sister's prowling instincts. Zee's face settled into an unattractive pout.

Cora could have hugged Simon, but instead she addressed the problem of her sister's invasion. "How did you find my address, Zee? How did you get into the building?"

"The address was on the return label to a gift you sent to Mother. A nondescript blouse." She shuddered. "And I walked in with guests of the party downstairs. I was just about to go down and crash the party. Who would have thought that my dowdy sister would be out on a date on Sunday evening? Isn't that against your religion or something?"

Simon edged forward so he now stood beside Cora, and his arm moved from her shoulders to her waist. "Is there another sister I haven't met, Cora? Who is this dowdy sister Zee refers to?"

Zee rolled her eyes. "Give me a break!" Her gaze snapped back to Cora. "I need a place to stay tonight."

"Not here. There are plenty of hotels in town. I'll drive you to one."

"I don't want to check into a hotel. Jim will find me."

"I don't know who Jim is, but I don't want him finding you here. And furthermore, the last time you stayed with me, you left with my hair dryer, my new coat, a pair of boots, and my MP3 player."

Zee's eyes grew wide. "You were robbed?"

"Yes. And the police recovered most of my things. *And* the description of the woman who pawned them matched *you.*"

Zee shook her head slowly. "What a coincidence."

"Yes, isn't it?" Cora looked up at Simon. "Would you carry her bag to my car? I'll drop her off at a hotel."

Zee stepped aside for Simon to get her suitcase, but she placed two hands on Cora's sleeve to make her plea. "I've changed, Cora. I really have. That's why I'm here. That's why I had to leave J—" Her voice broke, and she looked down for a moment. She lifted her chin and took a deep breath. "Jim. I want to know more about your Jesus."

"Good." Cora detached herself and started down the stairs. "There will be a Bible in the hotel. You can start reading tonight. I suggest the book of Ecclesiastes."

Zee alternated between a whine and a grumble all the way out to the parking lot. With one sentence, she claimed she was misunderstood. With the next, Zee accused Cora of having a judgmental attitude that would send her to hell.

Cora wasn't sure if her sister meant that Cora was destined to hell or if Cora's attitude would send Zee to hell. She didn't bother to interrupt her sister's tirade to ask.

As they walked to Cora's car, Zee turned her persuasive skills on Simon. "Surely you're a real Christian. My sister has never shared anything with me. Not one thing. Isn't that what Christians are supposed to do? She always thinks the worst of me. That's *not* what Christians are supposed to do, is it? Love your sister as yourself. I know I've heard that. Maybe it was brother."

"Neighbor." Cora unlocked her trunk. " 'Love your neighbor as yourself.'" *Oh, for pity's sake, she got me to respond. Watch it, Cora. You're not as practiced as you used to be. Ignoring her is your best defense.*

Zee brought out her lost-little-girl voice. She batted her eyelashes at Simon. "Why would God tell Cora to love her neighbor and not her sister? It just doesn't seem fair."

Cora looked up to see Simon smile kindly down at her conniving sister.

"Cora," he said, "perhaps we should spend some time with your sister. We could go to a diner and have coffee and explain some of the things she's confused about."

Cora marched around to the passenger side, unlocked the door, and held it open. "Get in, Zebra, before your stripes change to spots like the cat of prey that you are. Simon, you better go now. Thank you for the movie and dinner and carrying the Lost Wretch's suitcase, but you better let me deal with this snake in the grass. I know when she's about to sink her fangs in, and she's eyeing your jugular."

Zee laughed as she settled herself in the front seat. "Isn't Cora funny when she's mad?" She turned a smiling face to Simon and gave him a wave that consisted of three fingers wiggling.

Cora slammed the door shut and walked back toward Simon to go around the car.

He took her arm as she passed. "Don't you think we should give her the benefit of the doubt? It wouldn't hurt to get her something to eat and share the gospel with her before you drop her off at a hotel."

"Simon, I could probably produce a string of witnesses who could testify to the fact that it *does* hurt to give her the benefit of the doubt. The latest one would be this Jim, the J-Jim whose name she stumbled over because she wasn't quite sure what name she had given us."

"She's your sister."

"In our family tree, a lot of misplaced grafts came in the back door."

"Wouldn't Jesus say that Zee is one of the least of these and deserves to be loved and cared for?"

"Let go of my arm, Simon. I can't talk about this right now."

Simon's low, sincere voice scraped across her nerves. "Because you're afraid I'll persuade you to listen to your compassionate side?"

"No, because I'm about to use a karate punch on you. Let go!"

Simon dropped her arm, and she charged around to the driver's side. "Good night, Simon."

"I'll see you tomorrow. We'll talk."

Cora ducked into the car and muttered, "Maybe," as she clicked her seat belt in place.

Zee chuckled. "Now that was fun. Swing through a drive-through. I'm starved."

Cora switched on the ignition and backed out. Simon still stood on the sidewalk.

"Did you hear me?"

"Sure." Cora put the car in drive. "I'll even treat you. But that's it. You can stay in town if you want to, but you are not welcome in my life. Got it?"

"Sure," Zee purred.

Cora glanced at her sister's contented smile and felt her stomach twist into a knot.

13

Cora sat at her desk and did her best to clear off the Monday morning clutter. She refrained from turning completely around in her rolling office chair to get a good look at Mr. Serious Simon Derrick. For five years he'd walked past her desk with his day planner open and never looked her way. Last night he captured the attention of her heart. Today he blithely ignored her existence. He would be coming to dinner at her apartment tonight with Sandy. Would he be warm or distant?

A hand on her shoulder made her jump.

"Oh my goodness," said Mrs. Hudson. "I didn't mean to sneak up on you."

"It's all right. I'm afraid you caught me woolgathering."

"I'm not surprised, dear." Mrs. Hudson pulled up another rolling chair and sat beside Cora. "You're going to have a real Christmas this year. I'm so excited."

"I have a real Christmas every year."

"But as far as I can tell, you don't have a celebration."

"I celebrate."

"How?" Her supervisor leaned forward.

Cora leaned back. "I go to church, and…well, I have something special I do every year."

Mrs. Hudson scrutinized her through narrowed lids. "You aren't going to tell me, are you?"

Cora laughed. "No, I'm not."

The older woman straightened with a smile on her lips. "All right. But I do know you're going to the ball with Mr. Derrick and his sister." Mrs. Hudson winked. "So that's why you're woolgathering. And being slightly distracted by such a thing is perfectly natural. Simon Derrick is a handsome, kind man." She winked again.

Cora's eyes darted around the room, searching for anyone who might have overheard. She leaned closer and whispered. "I don't know if he likes me in a way that would lead to anything. And I haven't even figured out if I like him more than just…like." She scrunched her nose. "You know what I mean?"

Mrs. Hudson nodded. "I most certainly do. I raised five girls.

My Ginny used to say like, liker, likiest. Like a boy. Liker a boy a whole lot. Likiest him to pieces. After likiest came love."

Cora drew back and angled away from her supervisor. "Have you been sipping eggnog during breaks?"

Mrs. Hudson laughed and patted Cora's arm. "You missed the silliness of sisters and dating. And Dad scowling at your dates until beads of sweat popped out on their foreheads and their voices cracked."

"If I had dated when I still lived at home, my dad would have—" She caught herself and chose not to offer a glimpse of her home life. She forced a smile on her lips. "I e-mailed you the letter I composed to address the problems with the Midwest Hanger account. Have you had a chance to look it over?"

"Humph!" Mrs. Hudson stood. "I'll do it now." She frowned down at her. "Sometimes, Cora, you drain the color from a conversation. And I always wonder why."

Cora watched the woman walk away. That didn't go well. She'd poured turkey gravy on Mrs. Hudson's offer of cranberry cheesecake, ruining the camaraderie of the moment. Maybe she should have asked the older woman about her dinner with Simon and Sandy tonight. What should she expect? How should she act? Mrs. Hudson would probably enjoy the discussion.

She turned back to her desktop with a small frown.

"Focus," Simon's father said. Focus. She needed to focus and

not let her unpleasant family, mixed emotions about Simon—oops!—Mr. Derrick, and the lovely prospect of the ball keep muddling her thinking. Focus.

A crisis developed right before lunch, and Cora decided to eat at her desk. Tiffany, the office gossip, brought her a hot mug of tea and sat down to catch up on Cora's news.

"So Serious Simon Derrick is not married," Tiffany said as she leaned over her own cup of coffee, her eyes examining Cora's face.

Cora shrank back. This was going to be one of those times when talking to Tiffany would make Cora uneasy.

Tiffany sipped her coffee. "So…the 'family' he uses as a shield is not wife and kiddos, but more mom and pop and a sister?"

"Mother, Granddad, Aunt Mae, and sister, Sandy."

"I never would have guessed. He never flirts. And even some of the married men do that. So how'd you get through his defenses?"

"Just circumstances." Cora tried to busy herself with opening and closing e-mail windows. "And I wouldn't say I was favored to have a seat in the inner sanctum. He's totally ignoring me today."

"He ignores us all. It's his modus operandi. He does business with us and nothing more."

Cora sighed and looked around. Upper management was in a conference about the crisis. "But now I know he has a warmer side. And he even has a sense of humor."

Tiffany's eyes widened, and her eyebrows went up. "So this is turning into something more for you than just a chance encounter at a bookstore. Perhaps some romance at the Wizards' Christmas Ball?"

Cora flinched. Tiffany could do a lot of harm. She tilted her head and studied her co-worker. Tiffany was fun, but Cora made it a practice not to talk about her personal life much. Now she'd slipped up with the least trustworthy member of the staff. At least she hadn't referred to her plans for the evening.

Tiffany's next statement almost made Cora choke.

"It's not a sin, you know, to like one of the bosses." Tiffany frowned. "How are we single girls supposed to find the man of our dreams if the workplace is off limits?"

"Church?"

"I don't know about you, but our church is in the negative numbers when it comes to eligible bachelors."

Tiffany popped out of her seat and scurried back to work. Just then a couple of workers walked by, grumbling about a meeting. Tiffany was good at the hasty retreat. Cora would do well to emulate that behavior when tempted to discuss Simon and his family and her fluttering heart.

The mood in their office reflected the strain of too much to do before the holidays. A huge mix-up in the shipping department had to be dealt with that day or Christmas Eve deliveries would be impossible. Cora worked to remedy the situation and be sure her corner of the business world ran smoothly. Sorenby's didn't need any additional glitches.

By five o'clock a solution had been found, and the tension eased off. Co-workers laughed and parted company with a heightened sense of the vacation just around the corner. Cora closed down her computer and peered back at Simon's office.

"He's up on the executive floor." Mrs. Hudson informed her.

Cora jumped again. "What kind of shoes are you wearing?" she complained. "You never used to sneak up on me."

"It's not what I'm putting on my feet, but where your mind is wandering."

Her supervisor's voice sounded calm and pleasant, but Cora felt herself cringe. "Am I going to get a reprimand?"

"My goodness, girl, you always assume the worst." Mrs. Hudson sighed. "No, of course not. But you won't get a glimpse of Simon tonight. I'm hoping the executives are giving him the approval he deserves. He's the one who caught the error."

"Was it our fault?"

"No, but that wouldn't have mattered much if the delivery had been delayed until next week." She turned toward her desk and waved cheerily. "I'll race you to the parking garage. I don't want to spend one more minute at work. I have company coming for dinner."

Cora had company coming as well. Simon was to bring Sandy

over for a visit with the kittens. She was fixing spaghetti meat loaf at Sandy's request. Perhaps that wouldn't happen tonight, after all.

Her suspicion proved to be partially true. Sandy and Simon couldn't come until late in the evening, after dinner. Probably after eight. She would serve spaghetti meat loaf another time. Instead, she made dinner for one. Salad and a slab of fish microwaved and covered with a Cajun sauce. She picked at her cod and poked the fork in the salad. When she finally took a bite, she made sure she came up with a piece covered with dressing.

Neither Mrs. Hudson nor Tiffany thought an interoffice romance would rock Sorenby's. Cora admitted she felt more than just a casual interest in her supervisor's supervisor. He was very attractive outside the office and rather boring inside. His care for his family charmed her. But he was so different at work. She stabbed her fish and scooped up the tender morsel that flaked off.

The phone rang. Dropping her fork, she jumped up to answer. "Hello?"

"Howdy, Sis," Zee's voice greeted her.

Cora clenched her teeth and had to consciously force them apart to speak. "What is it?"

"Shouldn't that be 'Who is it?' "

"I know it's you, Zee. What do you want?"

"Your affection for me is astonishing."

Sharp words came too easily to her tongue. "Cut it out and get down to why you called."

"Just to tell you I've found a new love interest. I won't need to sponge off you. He'll take me under his wing and give me a free ride."

"Congratulations. Give me his name. I'll give him a call to warn him to hold on to his credit cards."

Zee's laugh sounded harsh and lasted too long. "I think not, Cora. When I leave, I like to have been of some value in a man's life. I teach them not only about of the pleasures of living but the dangers as well. You wouldn't want to spoil one of my favorite lessons, would you?"

"On the contrary, I'd be delighted." Cora placed a hand on her stomach. This familiar exchange of ugly comments made her sick. She had to snap out of it. She shouldn't be treating her sister like this.

Zee snorted. "You always were a prude."

"Was there anything else you wanted to discuss?"

"Just to wish you a Merry Christmas and to tell you I'll be moving on by New Year's."

Cora bit back the automatic response. "Zee, you know there's more to Christmas. Why don't you really make this year different and allow your heart to—"

The dial tone informed Cora that her sister didn't want to hear about Jesus. She tapped the End button and went to clear the table.

She knew better than to trade nasty remarks with her sister. She also knew better than to preach. Why couldn't she get anything right?

The weight of an early memory buckled her knees. She put the plate down on the table and collapsed into her chair. One night when she was nine and her sister Suzanne was six, Cora had held her all night long. The man who shared the house with their mother at the time raged from room to room in a drunken fury. Cora wedged herself and her sick sister between their twin bed and the wall.

Suzanne's fever rose. She whimpered and shivered. The sisters finally fell asleep. When Cora woke in the morning and Suzanne lay unmoving in her arms, she thought her sister had died.

Back then the prospect of death filled her with terror. Someone along the way had told her that life after death was just like life before, but much worse, and hell included lakes of fire, monsters that ate flesh, and unbearable noise.

After several years of Bible study, she had a better understanding of what hell would be like. Hell no longer had the power to scare her. She wouldn't be going there. But she still saw Suzanne as a sick child, needing the comfort and protection of Jesus.

Help me to pray for her.

The doorbell rang, and Cora got to her feet to answer.

Oh Lord, don't let that be her.

Ouch! I just asked to pray for her.

She put her eye to the peephole and let out a great sigh of relief. She opened the door and welcomed Sandy and Simon's mother.

"Simon couldn't make it after all," Mrs. Derrick said. "He had something he had to do tonight." She rushed over the words as if they'd been rehearsed. "I hope you don't mind that we still came."

"Of course not." Cora took their coats. "It's Sandy who wants to see the kittens. I'm not sure Simon is interested."

Sandy went straight to the cardboard box, knelt down, and spoke quietly to Skippy and her babies.

Mrs. Derrick smiled as she watched. Then she turned to Cora. "Simon is good with animals and has always loved dogs, cats, birds, lizards, and all the things little boys bring home."

Cora imagined Serious Simon with a frog cupped in his hands.

"And injured animals," continued his mother. "He had a knack for finding the wounded and bringing them home. I think if his father hadn't died, he would have been a veterinarian."

Cora frowned. What was the connection?

"Money, dear," Mrs. Derrick answered. "Even though we discouraged him to take the responsibility, he took on all his father's chores. And eventually Simon jumped into the role of breadwinner. My friend, who's a counselor, told me to let him. It was his way of dealing with his grief and something he needed to do."

Cora nodded slowly. She could understand that thinking. "I grabbed education as my life preserver. Once I got out of my family's house and started living with another family, the Bells, I imitated them right and left."

"Were they believers?"

"Mr. Bell made sure to present the plan of salvation." Cora laughed and deepened her voice to sound like a man. " 'For God so loved the world that he gave his one and only Son, that whoever believes in him shall not perish but have eternal life.' "

Mrs. Derrick smiled at the familiar verse. "And it worked, so it seems."

Cora laughed. "For about six months, I worked the plan of salvation. It was such a relief when I figured out the part about a free gift from God and no need to work for it. Somehow I had missed that point in Mr. Bell's presentation of the gospel."

"You aren't the only one who's made that mistake." Mrs. Derrick sat on the couch and accepted the kitten Sandy offered her. She held the tiny creature in her lap and used two fingers to stroke its back.

"Is it a girl or a boy?" asked Sandy.

Cora shrugged. "I have no idea. We'll ask the vet when we take them in for shots."

"Simon will take us," Sandy said. "He isn't always busy like tonight."

Mrs. Derrick made a motion at Sandy as if to stop her from speaking, but her daughter didn't see her.

"He got a phone call and had to go meet someone."

"Sandy," said Mrs. Derrick. "We shouldn't be talking about Simon's business."

Sandy turned wide eyes to her mom and shook her head. "It wasn't business, Mom. It was a lady named Zee. Isn't that a funny name?"

Mrs. Derrick bit her lips and cast Cora an apologetic look. "I don't know who this person is or what was so important that he had to see her tonight. Perhaps it's someone from church."

Cora forced her lips to part. She didn't want Simon's mother to read the anger and hurt that welled within her. "I know who it is."

Simon's mother sighed her relief. "Oh, then it is about work."

"Not exactly."

Cora busied herself with the kittens and Skippy. She became the perfect hostess and plied her guests with cookies and eggnog. Somehow she managed to keep a conversation going until Simon's mother and sister left. Then with fierce determination, she went through her nightly routine and put herself to bed.

Anger boiled through her, keeping her from shutting her eyes. She got up and picked a book from the shelf. A good novel, one about forgiveness. When she turned out the light after three in the morning, she quoted a verse to put herself to sleep. " 'In all things God works for the good of those who love him.' " *Does anything I do count for good?*

14

Cora gave thanks for the rush of the season. Busyness obscured the problems weighing on her mind. The office whirled with activity, and she only saw Simon once, and that was from a distance. She kept her nose pointed at her computer screen. When five-thirty rolled around, she'd done a record amount of data entry, tracked down two stray shipments, and solved a dozen or more pesky problems. She closed down her station, made a trip to the break room, and hustled toward the door. She didn't want to run into Simon.

In the crowded elevator at the end of the day, her co-workers traded festive banter. The anticipation of a few days off with family and friends injected a twist of humor into almost every exchange.

One more day at work, and most of her co-workers would be off from Christmas Eve until January 2. Cora smiled but couldn't bring herself to join in the excitement. The elevator doors opened, and with cheery good-byes, her co-workers went their own ways through the parking garage.

As she turned a corner in the dreary concrete-columned chamber, her heart sank at the sight of Simon leaning against his car. He looked like he'd been there awhile, with his arms folded over his chest and ankles crossed.

He straightened and plunged his hands into his pockets as she approached. "Mom called today and said Sandy told you about my meeting with Zee."

Cora nodded and pulled her keys out of her purse.

"I thought you might have misunderstood."

She nodded again. She wanted to say something, but her emotions paralyzed her vocal cords. Anger had dominated her reaction last night. Now she felt betrayed, both by her conniving sister and by this man who should have better judgment.

"She called the house and said you had given her my number."

Her throat relaxed. This trick sounded just like Suzanne hard at work, trying to cause as much trouble as possible. She probably just looked up the number in the phone book. How often had she fallen for her lines? Simon had no previous experience with her sister's winsome ways. She sighed and pointed out the obvious. "I don't have your home number."

"I figured that out later. And when I thought about what she said, I realized she had only implied that you had suggested we talk."

Cora looked at the cement floor. "Suzanne is gifted in expressing herself. She can make you believe anything. She manipulates people so they make conclusions that aren't based in reality. She makes them believe, but in her own twisted perception of the way she thinks things should be—the way Zee *wants* them to be."

Simon stepped closer and put his hand on her arm. His low, compassionate voice sent a shiver through her. "I realize that now."

She almost leaned into him, but he continued talking. "I still think we need to reach out and allow her to explore these new feelings of unworthiness. She may be ready to accept that she can't do everything on her own and invite God into her life."

Cora shook her head. "I've heard it all before."

"This time might be different. She asked some pointed questions last night."

"Simon." Cora sighed. "Suzanne worked for a small-time television evangelist. She knows the strings to pull, the buttons to push, the lingo to use. Preacher Bob was a charlatan, and he trained her well. She knows exactly what she's doing." She moved away from the comfort of his closeness to her car door.

Simon shifted from one foot to the other. "I'm supposed to meet with her again tonight, and Pastor Greg will be there. Would you come too?"

Cora jammed the key in the lock. "No."

"Give her a chance, Cora."

She swung the door open, threw her purse across to the passenger seat, and swiftly sat. "Just remember I warned you." She slammed the door and started the engine. She took deep breaths as she backed up. She didn't want to start bawling.

The drive home mercifully occupied her attention. She concentrated on the traffic. The snow and ice had melted, but every last-minute shopper in town raced over the roads in the wintery night.

"Go home," she yelled at the cars around her. "Spend time with your families. They're more important than any stupid errand could be."

She pulled into her apartment complex and sighed with relief. Her parking spot looked especially welcoming after that crazy swarm of vehicles on the freeway. Home, sanctuary, a bastion against the vagaries of a mixed-up world awaited her. Every step of the short walk to the front door of her building jarred loose some of the tension in her shoulders. But as she got closer, she saw a furry, orange, brown, and white something sitting on the stoop of the complex. Skippy wailed, then stood as soon as she saw her mistress.

"What are you doing out here?" Cora slipped her passkey into the slot and pushed the door open.

Skippy ran past her legs and up the stairs. She stopped midway, looked over her shoulder, and let out a harsh meow.

"I'm coming!"

Skippy paced in front of their door while Cora fumbled to insert the key and allow them inside. Skippy raced in, but Cora stood in the entry, reached over, and switched on the light. She caught her breath. The room was trashed. She pulled out her cell phone and dialed 911.

A policewoman walked through the apartment with a clipboard, taking notes as Cora listed the objects missing.

"Makeup, purses, several knickknacks, a few pieces of jewelry," said Officer Mann. "Most of these items are not worth much."

Cora raised her eyebrows.

The officer chuckled self-consciously. "That's no slur against you, Miss Crowder. Usually in a home break-in, the thief takes small, valuable items that will sell easily on the black market, like MP3 players, cameras, laptops. And they don't usually take the time to make such a mess." She cocked her head and narrowed her eyes. "That, with the lack of evidence of forced entry, would lead me to suspect the perpetrator is someone you know."

Cora winced. She'd avoided entertaining that possibility. Of course, her sister's proximity had prodded her to think the worst.

"You've thought of someone?" The officer waited.

Cora nodded. "But she doesn't have a key to the apartment. She's never been inside the front door."

"But she has been here?"

"Yes."

"It would be best if you gave me this person's name and how to contact her."

Cora rubbed her forehead with stiff fingers as if she could remove the headache that was her family. "My sister Suzanne. I have no idea what her last name is now. She was at the Fair-Roads Hotel on Buckertown Street two days ago. But I still can't see any way she could have gotten in."

"Do you have any idea why she would have been so destructive?"

"Looking for my credit cards." She saw the interest perk in the officer's eyes. "She knows I don't carry but one credit card at a time. She was looking for the other two."

"Obviously, you and your sister are estranged, yet she knows you have two credit cards hidden in the apartment?"

Cora shook her head. "Not two. Not the number. Just that I am likely to have some credit cards here rather than in my purse."

"And are they still here?"

"Yes, that was the first thing I checked for."

"Out of curiosity, where did you have them hidden?"

Cora tried a smile but was too weary to produce one. "In a pouch, tied to a string, suspended from the back of the refrigerator."

Officer Mann's head jerked back and her eyes opened wide. "Really?"

"She's stolen my credit cards before. As soon as I knew she was in town, I moved them from the desk drawer to a less likely place."

"Anything else missing in the bedroom?"

Cora slowly walked through the clutter on the floor. "I'll have to put some things away before I can tell for sure. She probably took some clothing." She opened the closet door. Everything hung neatly to the sides of a gaping hole in the line of clothing.

Cora gasped. "My dress is gone."

Officer Mann looked over her shoulder. "Was it valuable?"

"More valuable than the amount I paid." She felt tears welling up. "I got it for seventy-nine dollars. It was a ball gown. I'm going to the Wizards' Christmas Ball."

"Never heard of it." The policewoman gestured around. "It looks like she stopped here. This side of your room is ransacked. From the closet door on, everything is neat."

Cora closed her eyes and breathed deeply. "Maybe it was someone else. Maybe they heard a noise and got spooked."

"You don't believe that, Miss Crowder. We'll look for other suspects but will have to question your sister." She paused to give Cora a sympathetic look. "Don't feel guilty. You haven't put the finger on your sister. We always follow all leads and eliminate all possibilities. How does that sound?"

Cora squeezed her eyes tight. She managed to whisper, "Thank you."

"Laura," a voice called from the front of the apartment.

"Here." Officer Mann strode through the mess.

Cora followed, wishing she could back out of this scene and live someone else's life for a few days.

The other officer stood in her living room with the manager of the complex.

Why had the older gentleman felt it necessary to come in person? "Mr. Shepherd?"

He clenched his hands together. "Cora, it's my fault. I let her in. She had a picture in her wallet of you two when you were teens. She had a big package that she said was your Christmas gift, and she wanted to put it inside your apartment as a surprise."

"So you walked over and let her in?"

"Yes." His voice quavered, and he visibly trembled. "Yes, but I didn't leave her for a moment. Then we left. Together. I didn't think she had time to steal anything, but this policeman said she fixed the lock so she could get back in. I don't understand it, but he says she did it with a piece of tape. I can't tell you how sorry I am, Cora. Right before Christmas too. And she seemed so sweet and said how you'd practically raised her. And she said she loved you both as a sister and as a mother. She talked and talked." He shuddered. "I'm so sorry, and I suppose there's nothing I can do to make it better."

Cora sighed in frustration, more at how her sister had manipulated her landlord than his falling for her tricks. "I understand, Mr.

Shepherd. Please, don't blame yourself too much. She's very good at getting what she wants."

"Is she even your sister?"

Cora felt her jaw tighten and deliberately made her voice soft. "Yes. She is."

The telephone rang, and while Mr. Shepherd continued to remember details, Cora picked up the receiver. "Hello."

"Cora, it's Simon. I'm here with Greg Spencer, but Zee never showed up. I called the hotel, and she's checked out."

Cora's spirits lifted just a little. She could give Simon proof that he had wasted his concern on Suzanne. "That makes sense. She robbed my apartment this afternoon."

"She was caught robbing your place?"

"No, but the manager let her into my home so she could deliver a Christmas present."

"Did he see her take anything?"

"No, but—"

"Jumping to conclusions is never a good idea. Let's wait until we have more facts."

"There are plenty of facts!" Cora sputtered. Simon wanted to exonerate Suzanne. "You should see this place! There wasn't even a gift here that she claimed to be leaving."

"Maybe the thief took it."

Simon continued to spout his drivel. His excuses echoed the

ones her mother had always made for her youngest, prettiest, smartest daughter. Cora couldn't stand to hear one more word. She clenched her fist around the phone and held it away from her ear. When the faint noise on the line ceased, she pushed down the growl that formed in her throat and brought the phone back.

"Greg and I will come over," Simon said after the pause.

"No! Don't do that. I'm tired, and as soon as these police officers leave, I'm going to bed."

"All right, then."

He sounded put out. What right did he have to be upset?

He cleared his throat. "I'll see you tomorrow at work."

"Good night, and thank you for offering to come over."

"You're welcome. Good night."

Cora put down the receiver. That didn't go well. At least she remembered to thank him for his consideration instead of yelling at him for his stupidity. *Of course it was Suzanne. And he's going to see me tomorrow at work? Ha! More likely he's going to look right through me.*

"Miss Crowder?"

"Yes?" She looked up.

The two officers remained, but Mr. Shepherd had left.

"We're going to take a few fingerprints, then be out of your hair. Let's look at some of the things thrown to the floor. Can you pick out an object or two that are rarely handled? The perfect object would be something with a smooth surface that you cleaned thoroughly and just put back on the shelf."

In an hour the police were gone, and Cora sat on her bed, trying to decide what to do. She didn't want to go to work the next day. Simon wouldn't give her the time of day during work hours. The ball was the next night, and she had no dress. Her apartment looked like a tornado had swept through. Her charge cards were safe, but her heart wasn't.

Skippy jumped onto the bed. The cat had kept herself and her kittens hidden during all the commotion.

"What do you think, Skippy?" She picked her up and held her close. "Is this headache stress, or is my body trying to get me out of my obligations?"

Skippy purred in response to Cora's gentle stroking.

"No advice?" The cat wiggled enough to situate herself on Cora's lap. "Well, I would have listened to your advice, unlike some people who assume they know the way to handle my manipulative sister. And I trust you not to lecture me about being fair and not jumping to conclusions." She sighed. "I'm not going to work tomorrow, and I am not going to the ball."

15

Simon shrugged into the tight-fitting suit coat. A cutaway, that's what Bonnie Booterbaw called it. The front of the jacket came to his waist, the back hung down in tails. He buttoned the front over the fancy shirt, then studied himself in the mirror. Wiggling his eyebrows, he didn't bother to keep a goofy grin off his face. He actually looked pretty spiffy. At least Sandy would be impressed.

He frowned. Cora had called and talked to his mother. Of course, he'd known Cora had stayed home from work this morning. Mrs. Hudson told him she was cleaning up her apartment, filling out forms for the police, and generally trying to get her emotions stabilized. Mrs. Hudson twisted her hands as she also relayed Cora's message that she had no dress and no desire to go to the ball.

His mother confirmed this report. Both Mrs. Hudson and his mom had tried to persuade Cora that it would be better for her spirits to go to the ball with Sandy and Simon. She'd cried but remained firm. A ball was the last place she wanted to go.

Simon's mouth distorted into a jagged grimace reflected in the mirror. "Especially if it meant going with me."

Sandy's heavy tread thudded toward his bedroom. "Look at me, Simon."

He turned toward the door and gave his sister a genuine smile. "You look gorgeous."

Sandy grinned and revolved in place like a model. "Granddad and Aunt Mae have taught me dances. Can you do the monkey or the fox trot?"

He shook his head. "Maybe they should have been giving me lessons as well."

"You can dance. Mom told me."

"Did she tell you that Cora can't make it?"

Sandy hung her head, and a gigantic sigh almost deflated her. "Yes." She looked up at her brother with sad eyes. "Do you think we could go by her apartment and show her how fantastic we look?"

"I don't think Cora wants to see me."

Roiling storm clouds descended on Sandy's usual sunny expression. "Simon, what did you do?"

"I'm not sure, but I'm thinking about the possibilities."

Sandy's eyes narrowed, and Simon knew he was in for a lecture. "Call her, Simon. Call her. The Bible says—"

"I know what the Bible says."

"Then you know you should call her. If she's mad, you need to find out why and make amen."

"Amends."

"Do it."

Simon sat on his bed and picked up the phone. Funny, he'd already memorized her number from the few times he'd called about the kittens. Ha! No sense in trying to fool himself. He'd only called once about the kittens. After the first call, the kittens were only an excuse to see Cora.

"Hello." Her voice sounded sad, vulnerable, hurt. He was responsible for that somehow. "Hello," she repeated.

"Cora, it's Simon."

"Oh."

"Is there any way we can get you to go to the ball with us? With me?"

"No. Thanks for calling, but I'm really not in the mood."

Sandy poked him.

He cleared his throat. "What did I do?"

"Nothing."

"There had to be something."

"It's been a rough couple of weeks."

"How's that?"

"Okay. That's it. That's what you've done."

"What?"

"Simon, go to the ball. Have a good time. I just can't handle celibate cats giving birth, car accidents, trying to soften relatives' hard shells with Christmas presents"—her voice raised a notch and tightened—"sisters who manipulate my friends, and stupid wizards' dances."

Simon lived with three women—his mom, his aunt, and his sister. He recognized a female moment when he heard it.

"How about meeting me for breakfast tomorrow?"

"No." The phone went dead.

Sandy put a hand on his shoulder. "She's not coming?"

"No, she's not."

Their mother called from downstairs. "You two better get moving. Sandy, you promised not to give Simon a hard time and ruin the fun. Be a good girl."

"Yes ma'am," she called back, but she scrunched up her face and stuck out her tongue just before she turned and galumphed toward the stairs.

The radio broke the silence of the ride downtown, and about halfway to the hotel, Sandy began to sing along with the Christmas tunes. Simon tentatively joined her. When she didn't stop and give him the silent treatment, he knew she'd regained her positive outlook and that she would have a good time. But Cora was not having a good time tonight. And Simon realized he wouldn't have a good time either, knowing she was hurt and alone.

"Simon," Sandy said, "I'm going to spend Christmas with Cora."

"What do you mean?" Simon examined his sister's profile, trying to deduce what was going through her mind. "Did you invite her to our house? That would be great."

"No, I am going with her. She serves Christmas dinner downtown. And she wraps presents for kids."

"You better ask Mom about that."

"I'm twenty-four, Simon." Sandy gazed out the window for a moment. "You could come too. Maybe Mom, Granddad, and Aunt Mae too. Cora says she can't do things with her family because they don't treat Christmas with respect. But when she works at the shelter, she feels like she is serving people like her family, and it reminds her of God."

"Reminds her of God?"

"Yeah. God pulled her down one road because the other road would have led to the shelter."

"I see."

"Me too." Sandy hummed along with the radio.

Simon contemplated how hard it would be to follow Jesus if none of his family respected God.

When they reached Sage Street, they lined up with other cars following the guidance of costumed traffic directors. The men wore medieval attire and carried two flashlights each. One had an extended green cone over the lighted end, and the other had a red cone. Sandy watched the men wave their beacons, fascinated by the impromptu dance of colors.

Simon followed the car in front of him until guided into a ramshackle parking garage.

"I didn't notice this building when we were here before." Sandy craned her neck to see the shops close by. "This is the same corner. There's Michelle's candy shop."

"You had your eyes on the sweets and didn't notice this old building." Simon bit the inside of his lip. He didn't remember seeing this building either. Perhaps in daylight, he'd get a clearer picture and remember the three-tiered, concrete monstrosity.

"Do you suppose," Sandy said, awe in her voice, "that real wizards do things on Sage Street?"

"Like?"

"Like making buildings appear or disappear."

Impossible, but he paused to think about it. Was it really that outrageous? He knew better than to waste time on such speculation. He might never unravel the mysteries behind Sage Street. And did it really matter? No. Best leave it alone. This place was wreaking havoc with Simon's reason. But he couldn't help asking Sandy's opinion. "What do you think?"

"Nah." Sandy's head swiveled as she took in the interior of the dark warehouse with rows of parking spaces. "This place is odd. Look at the big pots over there."

"I think those are vats of some kind. It looks like this must have been converted from an old factory."

"The ball's not going to be in here, is it?"

"Definitely not. The Melchior Hotel is across the street."

Sandy bounced in her seat, and a rush of brotherly pleasure swept through Simon. He didn't often find exactly the right thing to make Sandy glow, but this ball had tickled his sister right down to her bones. They parked as directed by a man in a court jester's outfit.

Simon told her to stay until he came to open her door. "Hold your skirt up, Candy-Sandy." He helped her move the mountain of gauzy material around her legs so she could stand. "This is a cement garage floor and probably dirty."

Sandy stood and bounced on her toes. "Look at all the people, Simon. This is going to be so much fun."

Simon did look at the couples going toward the street exit, but he also looked at the cars they passed. The cars told more about the mixture of guests at the Wizards' Ball than the costumes they wore. After all, his old-fashioned cutaway tuxedo and his sister's extravagant pink princess gown didn't reflect the true Simon and Sandy Derrick. But his serviceable family car did. They passed minivans, older sedans, a few super-economy small cars, and a couple of SUVs. No upper-end, luxury models, and no sports cars were parked in the row of vehicles.

Another Wizards' Ball employee, dressed as a page, motioned

them toward the exit. On the street, Sandy gasped and pointed. "A red carpet. We're going to walk on a red carpet."

Both ends of the block were barricaded so no traffic cruised the street. A wide carpet paved the way from one curb to the other and then into the brightly lit doors of the Melchior Hotel.

"Ooh!" Sandy clapped her hands.

"Hold your skirt up until we reach the carpet. The sidewalk will be grimy."

She did as she was told. "I wish Cora was here. Maybe she'll surprise us. Maybe she'll be inside waiting for us."

Simon ignored the comment. Best to keep Sandy focused on the pleasure at hand and try to keep her mind off of Cora.

They stepped off the curb. "You can let go of your skirt now. This rug won't soil your dress."

Sandy did and promptly wound her arm around Simon's. "Cora'll be inside."

Simon clenched his jaw. "I doubt it, Candy-Sandy. Mrs. Hudson said she was firm about not coming. And she said no when I called."

"We should have gone by her apartment. I think if *you* had asked her in person, she would have come."

Simon didn't want to answer that. The idea of his making a personal plea hadn't even entered his mind. Why would she…? He took a deep breath. Maybe Cora liked him. He certainly liked her.

She loved Christ and was kind, thoughtful, vulnerable, sweet, and kissable.

He blinked hard. Yes, kissable. She looked like a good snuggler too. His face heated, and with a little more speed, he guided his sister toward their destination.

At the front door, William Wizbotterdad, dressed in elaborate wizard garb, sat on a high chair behind a podium, collecting tickets and assigning tables. He took the two tickets Simon offered.

"Simon Derrick, Miss Derrick." He checked his list and frowned. "There were three in your party. A Miss Cora Crowden?"

"Crowder," snapped Simon. He cleared his throat. "Miss Crowder could not make it tonight."

"I am so sorry." Looking disappointed, the bookshop owner handed them a six-inch round wooden placard with a golden number twelve painted on one side. "Here's your table number."

Simon smiled, trying to dispel the chill he felt coming from the host. "Sandy, this is Mr. Wizbotterdad from the bookshop. He's one of the sponsors of the ball."

Sandy made a little curtsy. "Pleased to meet you."

The old man relaxed and gave her a gentle smile. "And I am honored to meet Princess Sandy."

"Are you a real wizard?"

"Tonight I am as real a wizard as you are likely to meet anywhere."

Sandy giggled. "That's not a yes or a no, is it?"

William's eyes twinkled. He leaned forward and whispered. "That's a yes." He winked and turned to acknowledge the next couple entering the hotel.

As they moved on, Simon spotted a secretive, yet desperate, gesture by William Wizbotterdad. Bill Wizbotterdad came over, and an intense, whispered conversation ensued. They both looked up and caught Simon staring. The elder pressed his lips together and shook his head. What had Simon done to displease these characters? This was no time for borrowing trouble. Simon vowed to put all his attention and concentration on Sandy.

16

Cora sat on the floor with Skippy in her lap. The kittens climbed her legs as if they were scaling Mount Everest.

"We really should do something Christmasy," she told the feline family.

Maybe that would raise her spirits. She rubbed her furry friend's neck. Moping was not going to make anything better.

The cat twisted and presented her belly to be attended to.

Cora stroked the soft fur. "You're regaining your figure."

Skippy purred.

The kittens must have smelled milk, because they scrambled

toward their mother. She reluctantly rolled off her comfortable roost and allowed the babies to attach themselves for a snack.

Cora could bake cookies. But then she'd eat them. She could call a few friends for a quick Christmas greeting, but she'd end up telling them her tale of woe. "I'm all alone. My sister stole my dress. The love of my life is only the like of my life, and the promising beginning was railroaded by the same conniving sister. Woe is me."

She raked her hands through her hair. It was the kind of drama her family dished out. Who wanted to hear all that? She didn't even want to hear it. But she'd probably still be voicing the negative if she hadn't lived with the Bells. She needed a distraction.

Brownies! Christmas brownies. She could only eat half a pan of brownies. Much better for her than three dozen Christmas-tree cookies with colored icing and sprinkles.

In the kitchen she looked at the clock. Six forty-eight. She'd better eat dinner first, or she *would* eat the whole pan.

She opened the fridge. "Nada."

She opened the freezer. "Frozen chicken wings—buffalo or teriyaki? No thanks."

She reached for the pantry door, but the doorbell interrupted her browsing. *Who can that be? Simon? No, not Simon. Oh, not Zee! Please, not Zee.*

She smoothed down her straggly locks and batted at the cat hairs clinging to her sweats as she trudged through the apartment.

Through the peephole, Cora saw the distorted figures of Betty and Bonnie Booterbaw carrying a large bundle.

She opened the door. "Hello!"

"Christmas greetings, dear girl," said Betty as she pushed past Cora, dragging her sister and package along. "We discovered something absolutely disastrous, and we've come to make things right."

Winter cold clung to their thick coats.

"Please, come in."

"We're already in," said Bonnie. "Close the door before those kitties get out."

Cora closed the door. "Can I get you something warm to drink? Tea? Hot cocoa? Cider? How did you know about my kittens?"

"I can see the kittens, dear." Bonnie placed her end of the package on the seat of a stuffed chair, and Betty draped the other over the back.

"No time for a drink," said Betty. "You're already late for the ball."

Cora pointed at the long bundle. "That's a dress."

"Yes dear, and it's all our fault. We should have remembered about that fabric and time and unexpected properties."

"I don't understand."

Betty and Bonnie nodded in unison. Bonnie reached out and patted Cora's arm. "But we do, dear Cora, and we can fix it."

Betty clapped her hands together and said, "We must hustle. We have a driver downstairs to take us to the Wizards' Ball."

As they peeled off their coats, Cora tried to explain. "I'm not going."

Betty tossed her coat on the sofa where Skippy sat observing the new arrivals. The kittens ignored them completely. They had a toy with a bell to capture. The shopkeeper ripped the paper from the gown. The kittens perked their ears then and looked on with more interest.

Bonnie rushed to help her sister. "I'm not surprised! Your dress probably dissolved into tatters soon after it left the hanger. Age, you know, and disreputable—"

"Ahem!" Betty gave her sister a nudge.

"Fabric." Bonnie lifted the dress from the shambles of the paper bag, and Cora gasped.

The cats, mother and kitties, tackled the abandoned wrappings.

"It's gorgeous!" She reached trembling fingers to caress the soft gold satin. An underskirt of white velvet peeked out from beneath the draped satin. The scoop-necked bodice was a marvel of gold-threaded embroidery and beads on white satin brocade. Glittery trim accented the lines of the dress, and the sleeves billowed in a gossamer fabric down to tight three-inch cuffs that matched the bodice.

"Where's the hat? Where's the hat?" demanded Bonnie, looking over her shoulder. "Here!"

She held up a gold medieval cone hat. A veil of sparkling fabric matched the dress sleeves.

Cora put her hands over her mouth. "I can't. I can't do this. I don't have my ticket. My hair's a mess. I don't have a way to get there."

Betty put an arm around her shoulders and pushed her toward the bedroom. "I told you we have a driver downstairs. It's Bill Wizbotterdad from the bookstore. He's happy to drive us. It's an old-fashioned limousine. Almost a relic. Such fun to ride in and plenty of room for your dress."

Bonnie gently pushed her toward the bedroom. "We'll take care of everything."

"Yes dear," said Betty, "Bonnie is so good at fixing a hairdo, and I'll put on your nail polish. We brought shoes too."

"What if they don't fit?"

"Well, they aren't glass slippers so you don't have to worry about them breaking and getting slivers in your foot. I always said that was a nonsensical style, even for a ball."

Bonnie came up behind them with the dress. "They could do the slippers with acrylic now."

"But still," said Betty, "think what your toes would look like all squished together, and the sweat."

Bonnie let out a huge sigh. "Practical. Betty has always been the most practical of all the sisters. I prefer a little more fairy-tale perspective in my life. God has created such a fantastical world…"

Betty pushed Cora down to sit on her bed. "Oh yes. Like pearls from oysters."

"Or the blue morpho butterfly of South America." Bonnie clutched the dress and smiled. "A waterfall."

Betty thought for a moment. "The thoughtful expression in the eyes of a gentle burro."

"Fairies!" exclaimed Bonnie.

"Ahem!" The practical sister gave her an arched eyebrow. "We must get Cora ready."

Cora's emotions ricocheted, leaving her breathless, giggly, weepy, and confused. "Wait!"

"Wait?" asked Betty and Bonnie in unison.

"I...I have to decide if I want to go." She looked up at the two kind old ladies. "I'd decided it wouldn't be the end of the world if I didn't get to go. I don't *need* a night at a ball."

Bonnie took her hands. "Dear Cora, sometimes God gives us things we don't need. And the best of the gifts He gives us is someone to share all the silly and grand, frivolous and spectacular—"

Betty nodded solemnly. "—sad and heartbreaking—"

Bonnie's grip tightened on Cora's fingers. "—joyous and exquisite moments of our lives."

"You *really* think I should go?" Cora's voice quivered.

The two old ladies smiled and answered in unison, "Oh yes."

17

Elegant round tables surrounded the dance floor. Sandy matched their placard with the number on their table and bounced on her toes. Simon frowned at the beautiful decorations and the tableware set for three, while Sandy bubbled with enthusiasm. How did the organizers of this event know so much? It seemed they knew lots of details about the guests, whereas the guests knew very few about the ball. A ticket with no information, a Web site with no purchase details, last-minute e-mails with instructions—the whole thing was crazy.

Sandy giggled. "Look at the ostrich."

A big bird strutted through the crowd in front of them. The

people gasped in astonishment and readily cleared a path for the bird. The ostrich looked real, except for the cream colored feathers, iridescent with pink and purple. Simon squinted at the plumage. He shook his head and looked closer.

Although it moved with as much grace as any real ostrich he'd seen at the zoo, it had to be a mechanical bird. He suspected the organizers had borrowed it from some fancy movie special-effects department. The ostrich glided toward them. Sandy giggled nervously and backed up against her big brother. He put his arm around her.

"It's all right. It's only a—"

The bird stopped in front of them, stared Simon in the eye, looked at Sandy and made a soft, throaty noise, then moved on.

"I think she's real," said Sandy.

Simon swallowed the word 'robot' and nodded. "Let's sit down."

"There you are, Mrs. Finnfeather." A lady in a flowing golden wizard robe chased after the bird. "You promised to be good if I brought you along."

Simon and Sandy exchanged glances and burst into laughter.

As soon as they settled, a server appeared at Simon's elbow. His apparel was understated-wizard, rather than the flamboyant robes they'd seen on older gentlemen.

"Sir. Milady." He nodded toward Simon and then Sandy.

Sandy blushed.

"My name is Billy, and my pleasure is to ensure your delight in this evening's activities. Call upon me for any of your needs." He handed them each a small disk with a button marked "Billy."

Simon muttered his thanks as he examined the apparatus. Sandy pushed the button. The voice of a woman yodeling sounded from Billy. He grinned and reached into the breast pocket of his jacket. He held up a circle-shaped apparatus that had their number on it.

Billy clicked a switch and replaced his gadget. "Dinner is served at nine. The dance floor is open now, and the side rooms offer appetizers and beverages or games for your entertainment."

Simon nodded. "Thank you." He watched their server. "Are you Billy Wizbotterdad, the computer whiz?"

His eyebrows arched. "Yes, I am."

"Did you construct the Web site?"

Billy beamed. "That's my work."

Simon considered how to put his remark tactfully. "There are some holes in the information provided."

The young wizard put his hands up in a stop motion. "Not my call. I am only allowed to put up what the older wizards give me. They like to be mysterious, and I cater to their whims."

A mechanical voice sang an aria. He pulled out a different round apparatus, checked the number, and winked at Sandy. "Gotta run."

He scooted off before Simon could ask another question.

Sandy clasped her hands together. "This is going to be so much fun."

Simon guided his little sister toward the outer doors that led to a broad hallway circling the ballroom. "This is probably where they make their money, Sandy. I didn't bring a lot of cash with me, so we can probably only get a drink and something small to snack on while we wait for dinner."

"I don't mind, Simon. I'm having lots of fun. I wish Cora would come."

"I don't think she will. Remember? She doesn't have a dress."

"There's her dress." Sandy pointed down the hall. "See the fairy wings? I helped pick them, so I know."

Simon looked and spotted an azure blue gown with fairy wings. The woman wearing it passed into one of the side rooms before he could see her face, but her coloring and bearing strongly reminded him of Cora's sister.

Sandy grabbed his sleeve and hauled him down the corridor, dodging other guests. "Let's catch her."

The walls and ceiling of the passage sparkled with miniature Christmas tree lights. Tiny clear bulbs dotted a white textured substance.

"Ooh. It's like walking through a snow cave." Sandy paused to gaze at her surroundings. "It's sooo pretty." Then she jerked on Simon's arm. "Come on. Follow that dress!"

They turned into the side room and found carnival-type booths. Simon closed his mouth after a moment of surprise. The wizards had glitzed up many standard games. He saw traditional Skee-Ball, ringtoss, milk-jug bowling, a crane for scooping prizes out of an enclosed pile, and a spinning wheel. All performed the usual functions, but with much more style and sparkle than any arcade games Simon had ever seen.

"There she is." Sandy pulled Simon across the room as he got a glimpse of the back of the ball gown with fairy wings going through another door.

In the next room, hors d'oeuvres decorated round tables, and punch flowed from silver fountains. They caught up to the wearer of the dress.

"Zee," Simon addressed the young lady filling her plate with petite and pretty sandwiches. "I didn't know you were coming. Let me introduce my sister."

Zee swirled, the dress skirt spinning with her body and settling into lovely layers. She smiled. "Simon! How fortunate. I don't believe I've met one person here who wasn't firmly attached to a member of the opposite sex."

Simon refrained from pointing out that the purpose of the ball was for couples to have an enjoyable evening. "My sister, Sandy. Sandy, this is Cora's sister."

Zee's eyes slid to take in Sandy's face and went right back to Simon. "I'm so glad to be here. I believe I'll be sitting with you for dinner. We can continue the interesting conversation we started the other day."

"Cora's coming." Sandy's soft voice held a note of authority. "We can get another chair for you."

Zee's practiced laugh raked over Simon's nerves. "No, I know for a fact that my sister isn't coming. After all, she gave me her dress to wear and her ticket."

She extended her arm to emphasize the lovely gown. A patch of material dripped from the sleeve and floated to the floor. Zee frowned and grasped the fabric. She twisted the torn spot into her view. A handful of cloth came off, leaving a bigger hole.

Zee opened her fist and, with a look of disgust, examined the disintegrating swatch of blue in her hand. She wiggled her fingers, and fine powder poured off her palm. "What?"

"Uh-oh," said Sandy, pointing to the floor around Zee.

A ring of blue dust circled Cora's sister. The hem of her gown hung in tatters, losing more fabric with each move she made. Zee gasped and picked up her skirt. At the points where her fingers pinched the material, two strips of cloth fell to the floor. Her hands sprang back as if she'd been scorched.

Zee thrust her fingers into her hair. The beautiful concoction of gauze, feathers, and lace that crowned her head poofed into the air and showered down in a confetti cascade over her shoulders and gown.

"This is…this is… It's insane!" Zee spun around and raced for the door, trailed by blue dust. Palm-sized bits of fabric floated away from the train of her dress. Her wings drooped. Obviously her crowning moment at the ball had already passed.

"Is she going to be all right?" asked Sandy.

"I think so. She's probably mad. So much for the chicness of wearing an antique dress." Simon put an arm around Sandy's shoulders.

"It's magic," said Sandy.

"Magic?"

"That was Cora's dress, not hers. It was supposed to be on Cora, so it just fell off in bits and pieces. You shouldn't put a magical dress on the wrong person."

Simon studied his sister's solemn face. Sandy usually kept a level head and preferred factual explanations. She liked literal stories rather than make-believe. What was she thinking? Should he challenge this nonsense? No, he wanted his sister to have a good time.

But she wouldn't be totally happy. Cora was supposed to be with them. He knew what he needed to do.

"I'm going to go get Cora. Do you want to go with me?"

"Yes!"

As she donned each layer of her costume, Cora's excitement rose. A flexible hoop in the hem gave body to the satiny slip. As she twisted and twirled in her bedroom, the underskirt swayed and settled with a satisfying swish. Betty draped the swag of golden satin by hand, adjusting the height and flow of the material so that it accented

Cora's slim waist. The brocade bodice went on like a bolero jacket. Cora worked the multitude of tiny buttons into the fabric loops in front as she sat on a stool before her vanity. Bonnie styled her hair and secured the elaborate headdress.

Through the entire procedure, the shop owners chattered about former balls and the music they preferred. Of the two, Betty had a more classical bent in her tastes. Bonnie favored the big band sound of World War II.

"This gown will do well." Bonnie patted Cora's shoulder. "Whether you and Simon are dancing more sedate waltzes or shimmying to something with a little swing."

Bonnie's words had produced an odd stiffness in Cora's body, as if she'd been transformed into a waxen statue. Cora met her own eyes in the reflection of the mirror. She looked real enough, but she could well imagine this character, fashioned by the sisters' hands, in a painting or a historical diorama, like in a museum.

Except she didn't belong in a display, at a ball, or in Simon's arms. The last thought made her eyes widen, tears push at the back of her eyes, and a lump form in her throat.

"No, no, none of that," exclaimed Betty.

"You're a princess," declared Bonnie.

Cora snorted. "How do you come up with that?" Looking the part did not make her royalty.

Betty looked into the mirror, her eyes meeting Cora's. She spoke with solemnity. "We are children of God. We are also heirs—heirs of God and coheirs with Christ. And what would you call a child of a King?" She paused, cocked her head, and a twinkle sparkled in her eyes. She nodded. "A princess."

Cora didn't return her smile. "I'm a child of two drunks."

"You were, indeed. But since then, you were reborn into a royal family. Do not deny what God has given you. No matter who your earthly family is or how they failed you, your heavenly Father will never deny you nor forsake you. You are what you are, and He made you just so."

Cora took in a long, deep breath, then exhaled slowly. Cautiously she pulled her gaze away from the friendly old woman and examined her own image. Yes, she did look like royalty. She allowed herself to smile. She did feel special, like someone's cherished child, a princess.

She gave a nod to the young woman in the mirror. "Let's go."

18

Simon held Sandy's hand as they wove through the crowd.

"Excuse me, sir." Billy blocked their path. "It's time for Miss Derrick's photo."

Simon paused, irritated by the interruption. "I don't remember signing up for a photograph."

"Yes sir." Billy motioned toward a side hallway. "It generally takes ten minutes or less."

Simon said nothing.

Billy leaned forward and lowered his voice. "The photo shoot is part of the ball package. There's no extra charge."

Simon studied Sandy's face. She looked as undecided as he felt. "Sandy?"

Billy cleared his throat. "If Miss Derrick chooses not to have her picture taken now, her name will be moved to the end of the list, which means the next available time slot would be near midnight."

Sandy's eyebrows went up.

"Most probably, just a few minutes after." Billy admitted. "Well, during a few of the past balls, the last picture was taken around one-thirty, but that's not the norm."

"Sandy isn't much of a night owl." Simon put his hands on his sister's shoulders. "We could make this little side trip for the photographer and then go get Cora."

Sandy nodded. "Mom and Aunt Mae would like a picture and maybe Granddad too."

Impatience nearly got the best of him, but Simon put on a happy face. "It will just be a few minutes' delay."

They followed the young man down the hall to one of the last doors. Inside, they saw a room set up with photography backdrops. One section had an old-fashioned parlor ambiance. Another had a thick, plush, black cloth. A balustrade and painted night sky gave the illusion of an outside balcony. Another set looked much like snowy evergreen woods. Simon sniffed and noted a pine scent on the air as they passed. He glanced down and saw a stack of fresh-cut wood, then spotted a blazing fireplace that served as the last choice of backdrop.

He wondered how a real fireplace had been set up in a hotel room.

"Come in, come in," instructed a small man, wearing black slacks, a black turtleneck, and black shoes. "I am C'Maine, an artist of film. You are Miss Derrick." He frowned at Simon. "My notes say this is a single portrait. Would you like to be in the picture?"

"No, this is Sandy's night. I'm content to watch. Um, we are in a hurry."

"Yes, yes, the hurry." C'Maine came forward and took Sandy's hand, drawing her to the center of the room. "Sandy Derrick, I am charmed to meet you. Your dress is exquisite. May I suggest a shot with the plain background first? That helps me to test the lovely image you project in your costume." He turned to Simon and pointed to a bench by the wall. "You may sit there."

"Don't forget," said Simon as he sat on his designated spot, "we have to leave soon. We're picking up a friend."

"Of course. I understand the hurry." C'Maine gave Simon a dismissive nod, then beamed at Sandy. "Your complexion is angelic. Pale with just the right blush of pink, like the petals of a glorious rose."

Simon rolled his eyes and rested his back against the wall. The man's accent was sliding all over Europe. But Sandy was eating up the flattery.

The photographer's attention was solely on Sandy. "Please, come stand here. So."

He took a moment to pose Sandy and flick the folds of her dress into an attractive drape, then went to his camera and looked through the lens. "Something is not right."

After pulling his head back, he frowned, then looked again. "A shadow that should not be." He strode to Sandy's side and turned to study the bank of lights. "Aha! 'Tis simple. I must replace a bulb." He clicked his heels and gave a quick bow to Sandy. "A minute, you must wait. I apologize. Please, sit with your brother. I do not want the flower to wilt in the blazing lights." He shooed her off the set.

Sandy plopped down next to Simon, her eyes wide and sparkling. "I'm the flower that will wilt in the lights, Simon. This is fun!"

Simon deliberately smiled at her to mask his growing frustration. "This is pretty fantastic, isn't it?"

She nodded, busy examining all the nooks and crannies of the crowded room.

"Sandy, I'm going to step out and call Cora on my cell."

"Okay."

"You'll be all right?"

"Yeah."

He patted her hand and headed for the hall.

The door opened as he got there, and Billy jerked back as though startled to see him. "Where are you going?"

Tension put an edge on Simon's tone. "To make a phone call."

"But you can't. It's against policy."

"Making a phone call is against policy? What kind of policy is that?"

"No sir. Excuse me. I meant it is against policy to leave a young female guest alone with one of our male employees." He peeked around Simon's solid form and waved at Sandy. "We like to protect young ladies from what might be an awkward situation. A chaperone, in the old-fashioned sense of the word, is needed."

C'Maine called out as he climbed down the stepladder. "The old light bulb is gone. The new beams upon us. Come, my young subject. Pose and we shall be done."

Sandy jumped up and returned to her position. C'Maine made a few adjustments to Sandy's dress and the line of her elbow.

"A masterpiece," he muttered as he again gazed through his camera. A series of clicks, as he rolled the apparatus closer and then to each side, testified to a great number of images being collected.

He gave a thumbs-up to Sandy. "You may relax. Please choose one other background. To complement your dress, I suggest, with my eye of an artist, the parlor or the balcony."

The man went to work rearranging his bank of cameras.

Simon sighed as he stepped forward. He might as well help, or it would take forever to get this quick photo done. He tripped as his foot caught on a cable, but he recovered enough to avoid decking an expensive-looking camera on a tripod. He counted himself blessed until he heard C'Maine sharply utter some foreign phrase that did not bode well. Simon glanced up and saw that his clumsiness had dislodged several reflector panels, which were part of the elaborate lighting of the studio, from their moorings.

"Bird!" exclaimed C'Maine.

At the same time, Billy yelled, "Duck!"

Heavy sheets of shiny material swooped down into the center of the room.

Simon watched in horror as the panels leaned in. How could an electrical cable yank the moorings of the giant reflector sheets?

Sandy screamed. They all covered their heads and crouched close to the floor. The giant reflectors swung back and forth. Slowly the speed and scope of the dangling menace lessened. Sandy straightened and searched for her brother. "Simon, are you all right? Mr. C'Maine?"

Simon appeared from behind a screen. "I'm fine, Sandy."

"Alas!" said C'Maine as he dodged a gently swaying reflector. "The diffused lighting is kaput."

"Well, then." Simon cleared his throat. "Perhaps Sandy and I should leave while you put them in their proper places. We're obviously in the way."

"Not a problem," said the cheerful photographer. "You must stay. Never has C'Maine failed to please a client." He pointed to the ceiling. "A knot, maybe three, and the light panels, they all hang in their proper places. You must not feel bad, Mr. Simon Derrick. Only a misfortune. Delays us two, three minutes. Billy, you are to grab the boom arm and attach this like this and that like that." He demonstrated as he spoke.

"We really must go," Simon explained. "We want to pick up a friend so she can come to the ball."

"Miss Derrick, parlor or balcony? Your brother is in a hurry."

"Balcony."

"Excellent choice. Now I know how these dangling light panels must be in positioned. You, beautiful princess, sit. Brother Simon, friend Billy, and I will fix this accident of misfortune."

Simon figured it would be quicker to help than argue. He followed C'Maine's instructions, and the light reflectors soon hung just as the photographer desired.

"You are so patient, Miss Sandy." C'Maine maneuvered her back in place. "I commend you."

By the time C'Maine clicked a hundred or more pictures, Simon held on to his patience by the last hair on the tail of a stubborn pig. He wanted out of there. With barely a gracious word to the artist, he grabbed Sandy and propelled her toward the hotel lobby.

Billy dogged their steps as he explained how they would pick up the photos later that evening, then rushed ahead to the large glass doors at the entrance. Simon readied himself to pick up the pest and bodily move him aside if he tried to delay them one more time. But as they approached, a server opened the door and bowed them through.

Sandy pointed. "A limousine!"

Parked across the red carpet, a long, sleek, and very, very old black limo blocked their way.

Simon gritted his teeth. "We'll just go around."

"Simon, wait! Look!" Sandy tugged away from his iron grasp.

Betty Booterbaw stood by one of the back doors. Bonnie emerged next. They wore elaborate gowns from their store. The next passenger leaned forward and came into sight. A tall, glittering, cone-shaped hat pointed out of the passenger door.

Simon heard Sandy catch her breath. "She's a real princess."

"I don't—"

"Maybe a fairy princess!"

"Sandy, there are no real fairy princesses. That's just someone else who got her dress from the Booterbaw Costume Shoppe."

From the shadows of the street, a figure charged toward the car. Her high-pitched screech galvanized several men standing nearby into motion. Simon left Sandy's side and placed himself between the new arrivals and the harpy whizzing their way. Two more men intercepted the woman and held her as she struggled wildly.

"My dress," she wailed. "You ruined my dress."

Simon gaped at the woman shrouded in dull gray rags. Zee fumed, kicking her captors and uttering oaths. Even with rage snarling her face, Simon felt compassion for Cora's sister. But her tirade opened a well of protectiveness for the quiet young woman from his office. Whenever they *finally* reached the apartment, he intended to wrap his arms around Cora and vow to keep her safe.

Betty and Bonnie Booterbaw flanked Simon. Disapproval flowed between them. Simon drew back as he felt an almost tangible cold barrier form in front of him.

Zee renewed her struggle to get loose. "You're part of this, aren't you?" She sneered at the women. "You're all on her side. You've ruined me."

"Nonsense, girl," said Betty. "Your greed eats away your pleasure."

Bonnie nodded. "Your dishonesty tarnishes all you possess. One of our dresses was bound to fall to pieces on someone unworthy."

"Unworthy!" Zee strained against the arms that held her. "You can't judge me. Nobody judges me, because I don't give them the chance."

The Booterbaw sisters looked past Simon at each other and each gave a smart nod.

"She would be a challenging project," said Betty.

"Almost beyond our powers," agreed Bonnie.

"Not almost, sister. I believe this project is irrefutably beyond our ability."

Bonnie's eyebrows shot up. "Oh, what a blessing. I love it when He has to help us out because the job is too big. Can we begin tonight? Our work for the ball is done."

Betty gestured to the men holding Zee. "Put her in the limousine, and we'll take her for a nice cup of tea."

Simon stood aside, vaguely aware that Sandy had come up behind him and beside the mysterious woman who'd arrived in the long black car. Eyes widened with curiosity, Sandy watched all the different players of the silly drama.

Under the soothing chatter of the old ladies, Zee calmed down. "Tea?" she whimpered. "You're giving me tea?" She looked Betty in the eye and summoned a tentative protest. "I don't want tea."

Bonnie patted her arm. "Tea with cream. And some sweets. Little cakes and some sandwiches. You're probably hungry."

Betty moved closer and wrapped her arm around Zee's middle. "Goodness, you must be cold. Come. We'll find you something warm to wear."

As the sisters persuaded the reluctant but noncombative waif in tatters into the limousine, Simon reached for Sandy's hand.

"Come on, Sandy. If we hurry, we can still make it."

"Simon?"

Sandy dragged her heels, but Simon wanted to get to Cora. He pulled his sister along the sidewalk and stepped off the curb behind the long car.

"Simon, we don't have to go."

He turned to gaze into his sister's troubled eyes. "I have to go, Candy-Sandy. I don't want to disappoint you, but this is about being where God wants me for the rest of my life, not just tonight."

"Are you sure?"

"Very."

Sandy grinned and looked over her shoulder at the few people still standing on the red carpet in front of the Melchior Hotel. Simon followed her gaze.

The passenger from the limousine faced them, her hair swept up under an impossibly tall medieval hat. A sparkling veil trailed from the tip and covered her shoulders, framing her face.

As Simon pulled in a long, slow breath, warmth spread through his limbs, and his heart thumped inside his chest until he knew everyone around could hear.

Cora, a vision, stepped forward. "Where are you going in such a hurry?"

"To find you." He took her hands in his and pulled her closer.

"Why?"

"Because I suddenly realized I've been looking for you for a very long time." He kissed the back of one of her hands, then the other. He let go, then encircled her waist and closed the small gap between them. She tilted her chin up, gazing into his eyes, and he took that small token as encouragement for a much more satisfying kiss.

The limo engine started, and the car eased away from the curb. Cora pulled back from Simon and stared at the departing vehicle. "Will Zee be all right?"

"You're worried about Zee?"

"She's my sister."

"But?"

"I believe I finally caught the spirit of Christmas."

Sandy moved closer to her brother and Cora. "You did? How?"

"Betty Booterbaw said, 'No matter who your earthly family is or how they failed you, your heavenly Father will never deny you nor forsake you.' That made me think about why Jesus was born."

" 'Because he will save his people from their sins,' " Sandy recited with a grin.

"Yes," Cora agreed. She let go of Simon's arm to reach out and touch his sister's hand. "He came to those who failed our heavenly Father. He didn't run away from them but came to them. He *went* to them. I thought my family had failed me, so I ran away. But it's time to put the past behind, where it belongs, stop judging and resenting them, and just offer love."

"And that's the Christmas spirit?"

Cora chuckled and leaned her head on Simon's strong chest. "The Christmas spirit is giving what you already have, not going out to find something to buy."

"But I like to give presents."

"That's because you are giving from what you already have. The gift is a symbol of respect, love, honor. And that's what you have."

Simon hugged Cora tighter. "You're a gift to me."

Sandy made a face. "But I don't like Zee."

Simon glanced at his sister. "We don't like what she does, but that doesn't mean we stop loving her."

Cora frowned. "That is going to be hard, very hard."

"I know you can do it. We'll help." He captured her lips once more.

Beside them, Sandy sighed.

"Miss Derrick?" Billy stood at her elbow.

Sandy looked at the server. She waved an admonishing finger in his face and chided him. "You were keeping us here on purpose, weren't you?"

He grinned. "I knew the Booterbaw sisters had been sent to get Miss Crowder, and if you left, you might pass them as they were coming here."

"That was very sneaky." She put her hands over her mouth as she giggled. "I like this ball. I like wizards."

Billy studied her for a moment. "You have it all figured out, don't you?"

She nodded.

He presented his arm. "May I escort you to the ballroom? I would very much like to dance with you."

"Is that allowed?" asked Sandy. "I mean…"

"Is an employee allowed to dance with a guest?" Billy winked. "At the Wizards' Christmas Ball, Princess Sandy, you can dance with whomever you please. Even a humble servant."

Sandy giggled. "Do you know the fox trot?"

He nodded. Sandy grabbed his arm and tapped Simon as they passed him and Cora. "Come on, we're going to monkey and fox trot."

Billy whispered, "Maybe we can invent the monkey trot."

Simon looked into Cora's eyes. "Miss Crowder, will you come to the Wizards' Ball with me and do the fox trot?"

Doubt etched a grimace on Cora's face. "Fox trot? You're going to have to help me with that one too."

Simon grinned. "My pleasure."

Acknowledgments

God is so good to give me pushers and prodders,
supporters and cheerleaders!

Mary Agius

Jessica Barnes

James Matthew Byers

Evangeline Denmark

Jani Dick

Jack Hagar

Jim Hart

Kathy Hurst

Heidi Likens

Joel Kneedler

Shannon Marchese

Shannon McNear

Carol Reinsma

Faye Spieker

Tiffany and Stuart Stockton

Case Tompkins

Beth and Robert Vogt

Kim Woodhouse

Laura Wright

And a special thanks to Dianna Gay,
who swooped in and saved my sanity.

About the Author

Donita K. Paul is a retired teacher and the author of numerous novellas, short stories, and nine novels, including the best-selling DragonKeeper chronicles, a series which has sold more than 350,000 copies. The winner of multiple awards, she lives in Colorado Springs, Colorado, where she enjoys the fellowship of other writers and is active in promoting literacy for the next generation.